Romancing the Wrangler

SARAH LAMB

Contents

Dedication		1
1.	Chapter 1	3
2.	Chapter 2	11
3.	Chapter 3	19
4.	Chapter 4	27
5.	Chapter 5	31
6.	Chapter 6	37
7.	Chapter 7	43
8.	Chapter 8	47
9.	Chapter 9	47
10.	Chapter 10	47
11.	Chapter 11	47

12. Chapter 12   47

13. Chapter 13   47

14. Chapter 14   47

15. Chapter 15   47

16. Chapter 16   47

17. Chapter 17   47

18. Chapter 18   47

19. Chapter 19   47

20. Chapter 20   47

21. Chapter 21   47

22. Epilogue   47

Note from Author   47

About the Author   47

There are other great books in this series as   47
well!

Dedication

To Nancy and Cheryl, for taking the time to answer my
questions endlessly and supporting me as an author.
I am so grateful for you and your guidance.

Chapter 1

1885, Oregon

Rose Alden tiptoed past her father's study, careful to not scuff her boots and make a noise. Some of the floorboards, though covered by a carpet with flowery scrolls running down the middle, were old and made creaking sounds.

As a young girl, she'd quickly learned which areas to avoid to prevent the unwelcome sounds, but as she grew, it seemed so did the number of boards that groaned when stepped on.

Inside, she could hear her parents talking. She *had* fully intended to sneak up the stairs and to her room to read for a while before dinner, when she'd heard her name.

While it would have been polite to continue past, her curiosity got the best of her. *If they didn't want me to take notice of their conversation, perhaps Father shouldn't have said my name so loudly,* she told herself.

Freezing, as she heard her name once more, she moved closer to the door. Yes, she knew she shouldn't be eavesdropping, but if it was something about her, didn't she have every right to know what it was? And her parents, being the way they were, likely were not even going to let her know what it was they were talking about until it was too late to react in any way.

"...running out of chances," her father's frustrated voice said.

Chances? For what? Rose frowned. The thick wooden door muffled some of the words.

"Which is why...accept. We both agree that...eligible. And wealthy." Her mother's voice, though muffled, still had a tone of smugness.

"Invite him for dinner," her father said. "...fine match. Rose will be pleased."

Stiffening, Rose clenched her fists as she straightened. Her shoulders ached with the sudden tension running through her, and her head started to throb. No, Rose would not be pleased. Rose didn't want to be told who to marry. And Rose didn't intend to marry. At least, not right now.

It was all she could do not to burst through the door, her jaw clenched, and let her parents know exactly what she thought about their plans. The plans she wasn't supposed to know about. Rose took a breath to try and calm herself. Then counted backwards from ten. Neither helped.

Marriage. She wasn't wanting marriage. There was so much of the world out there to explore and see. So many things she wanted to do, and she didn't want anyone telling her she couldn't do those things, simply because she was a woman. While yes, that would happen in or outside of a marriage, being wed would also mean fewer opportunities to do the things she longed to do.

I'm as capable as anyone, she fumed. Then her shoulders slumped. It didn't matter. The topic of her independence and desire to be more than simply a woman and a wife was a conversation she'd tried to have many times, and one her parents finally put a stop to. She was a daughter, they reminded her, she had no rights and no say, and was to obey.

That wasn't something she wanted. What was wrong with making her own way in the world? She could! Rose was sure of it. Other women did.

"...Rose. A fine...agree." Her mother's voice was incredibly faint.

Rose listened as hard as she could, her eyes narrowed in concentration, hoping to discover the man's name her parents wished to bind her to, but her parents must have moved across the room. She couldn't hear anything now.

However, the sound of footsteps nearing from the foyer was loud and clear. While she didn't know who it was walking her way, she also didn't intend to find out. Rose straightened, swiftly moving over the floorboards with little effort to avoid the noisy ones, and slipped up to her room, easing the door closed behind her.

Taking a deep breath, she stood, her back pressed to her door. Her parents' words were sinking in, and the initial shock was gone. Invisible chains seemed to clamp around her, and Rose looked down at her hands, almost as if she could see them. Rose gulped in a second breath, trying to stay calm, but it didn't help. Her chest rose and fell heavily, and she felt as though she was suffocating. It was too warm, and she felt a little lightheaded. She opened her window and stuck her head out, drinking in the fresh air.

Beyond her room, birds sang somewhere, a gentle breeze made the tall oak tree branches sway, and beautiful flowers, all in pinks and whites, in her mother's garden bloomed. Their scent wafted into her room. It was a paradise outside. Inside, a prison. The only thing missing from her life were the bars. But perhaps her parents would add those. She didn't doubt it. It really was all that was missing from her existence.

Rose paused her thoughts, reconsidering. Perhaps she was being too dramatic. Her parents loved her, she was sure. But they also loved being well off, and making connections to improve their status and advantages in life. With her an easy offering, of course they planned to use her to do that. All under the guise of Rose doing her duty and having an *opportunity*.

There was a knock on her door. Startled, she quickly snapped herself out of her thoughts. "Come in," she called, as she sat next to her window and snatched up a nearby book.

Her mother strode in, glancing around. "Rose, dear, we are having a guest for dinner tomorrow," she said, walking to Rose's closet. She flipped through the dresses that hung neatly, creating a rainbow in their order, considering several before she spoke again.

"You'll wear the mauve gown, have your hair half up, half down, curled along your face, and the new slippers I got you last week. No jewelry. You can't help being plain looking, but we don't need to showcase that with jewelry. You are to appear innocent and mild." Her mother looked at her then, fixing her with a sharp gaze. "That is how your tongue is to be as well. Do you understand?"

"Yes, Mother," Rose answered, swallowing back the sting of her mother's words.

It was true, she wasn't beautiful. But did her own mother have to remind her of it so often? Her hair, long and dark, was a glory. But her skin was too pale, her body perhaps a little thick for her mother's liking, though it wasn't an excess of food, but muscle.

She took after her father, and was more so sturdy than petite. Sometimes it bothered her. She'd love to float through a room in an airy dress, not lumber her way through because she was a little clumsy.

And for her tongue? She couldn't help it; she had a quick wit and sometimes spoke before thinking. While she did try to be mild-mannered, too often she wasn't. Why should she feel guilty for that? Couldn't she be herself? The thought made her want to scowl, but that would be criticized as well.

Pressing her lips together, Rose took her eyes from her small mirror. Right now, she didn't care much for the young woman she saw staring back at her. What man would? He would have to be something different, something unusual and unlike most of those she'd known, if he was to like her for herself. Was there such a man? It seemed unlikely.

Then, she risked asking, "Who is coming?"

Her mother's face changed then. Her eyes lit, her hands clasped together as she brought them to her chest, and she exclaimed, "Mr. Douglas West."

"And he is coming to do business with father?" Rose asked hopefully.

"In a way." Her mother giggled then and a shrewd expression formed. "You, being his business, dear." She strode to Rose's bedroom door. "So much to do to prepare. I'm headed to the kitchen now to see a proper meal is prepared." She swept out without another word.

Standing by the open door, Rose listened to her mother's footsteps fade. Once she was sure her mother wouldn't return, perhaps having forgotten to tell her something like which bath soap to use or some other thing she deemed important to manage, she slipped back downstairs and through a servant's door leading outside. There she ran to the one place she knew she could find comfort from her hurt and anger.

Hurrying along the dirt path about a hundred yards from the main, wider path leading to and from the house, she paused, staring at the large barn before her. Just beyond the door stood the thing to take her to what she wanted most.

Freedom.

Rose slipped in through the open barn door and made her way down the row of horses. They'd been recently groomed, she could see. It would have been easier to take one of the horses from the field, she could ride bareback, but it would be a longer walk and she might be seen by her father. He didn't like her riding without a saddle, and he never let her ride alone.

Besides, if she did, she wouldn't be on her horse. Gifted to her for her thirteenth birthday, Ruby was all she'd longed for, and who she told all of her secrets to.

Rose unlatched the door and entered the stall where her horse waited. Ruby stood tall, a deep red hue, and nuzzled Rose with her nose. "Hello, girl," Rose said, and then wrapped her arms around her horse's neck. After a moment of letting herself breathe in the familiar scent of her friend, she pulled back. Slipping a halter around Ruby, she planned to just take her out for a quick ride. A saddle would be more comfortable, but again, she could be caught with as long as it would take to put it on. Bareback would do.

Of course, her mother would have a fit, it wasn't ladylike at all, but that fact was all the more reason to slip out before anyone could see her.

The halter on Ruby, Rose unlatched the stable door. She led the horse toward the door, when a large man with muscular arms crossed over his chest blocked her path, and growled, "Do you know what they do to horse thieves?"

Chapter 2

Levi Patterson helped himself to another serving of beans, jerky, a slightly wizened apple, and a biscuit. The man cooking for the cowboys called out, "More water or coffee?"

With a headshake, Levi held up his cup. "Still have plenty, Jim, thanks," he told the man.

"Ain't much of a cook," Jim said, by way of apology. "Weren't why I was hired, neither."

"Same," Levi said. "Though I suspect you're better at it than me." He let his eyes roam over the cattle and the horses a short distance away. After satisfying himself they were all there, including the pregnant mare his boss was most concerned about, he asked, "What can you tell me about Mr. Alden? Only met him when he hired me, and that's about it. My week there before we left, I didn't see him again. I'd like to know a little more about what I've gotten myself into."

Jim tugged at his chin, where a scruffy salt and pepper beard had formed over the last two weeks. "He's firm but fair with his hands," he started. "Expects a lot, but pays well. I suspect you can't ask for better than that."

"Saw his wife once," Levi said.

Before he could say anything else, Jim slapped his knee and laughed. "Something else, that one. Voice so shrill and demanding, makes me wonder why he ever married her."

A cowboy called from across the snapping campfire, "You know why. She had just as much money as he did. Those two care only about one thing."

"What's that?" Levi asked, taking a bite. He didn't put all his stock in gossip, but sometimes that was the only way to learn more about a person, or who you were working for.

"Status," Jim said, with a slow and mournful headshake. "Married off their first daughter to a man just as wealthy as they were. Did the same with the second. They've been trying to do that to their youngest. I suspect it galls Mr. Alden it hasn't happened yet."

"Why not?" Levi asked. "I saw her once from a distance before we rode out. She's not bad looking."

"Not because of her looks," Jim explained, "Though she takes after her father, a little on the plain side. No, it's her. She's not fussy, like some. The girl's got gumption.

Always has. I taught her to ride," he said, gesturing to the horses, "but then her parents got real concerned it wasn't becoming of a young woman of her status to be around the barn so much. They didn't care for her wit, neither. She's got a sharp mind, speaks it too, and has put all the men interested in her into their places. Her parents don't like that. By this point, they must figure no one will want to marry that kind of trouble, and it doesn't help improve their standing."

Levi snorted. "We're in the West. Sure, some people have money, but status? Isn't that why most of us are here? To get away from that, to enjoy life and have a little freedom?" He gestured to the dark sky above, lit by a bright moon and dotted with stars.

"You'd think," Jim agreed. "Still, there are always a few in every town, and with the railroads now, makes it easier for those fancy folks to travel around and find each other."

"And keep their fancy folk circles," someone, Levi couldn't see who, joked across the fire. "It's a lot like wagons on the trail circling the livestock for protection. They don't like to give up what's theirs, only make it bigger."

There was some general agreement, then one of the cowboys pulled out his guitar, and everyone fell silent listening to him strum. Levi contemplated all Jim had said. He wondered what Mr. Alden's daughter was like. It couldn't be easy, being of a different mind than her father.

That was one thing they had in common. He doubted there was anything else, not a rich girl like her. Nope, he'd given all that up, left it behind, and he was glad. Good riddance to that life, the people, the expectations. He wasn't planning to return to any of it.

Levi performed one more check on the horses, made sure they were tethered tightly, and then leaned back on his bedroll and shut his eyes, having been given the third watch. The next morning, after the sun rose and they broke their fast, they rode back to the Alden ranch, the cattle and horses they'd purchased all safe.

The horses his responsibility, and his only, Levi and the young stable boy, Billy, led them to the large barn and stalls, where Levi made sure each had feed and water, and were comfortable.

After caring for the animals, he headed back to the bunkhouse. A hand he'd never seen before pushed past him in haste. Levi meant to ask Jim who it was, but he'd forgotten when he saw the letter on his bunk. He hadn't had time to read it then, not with the other men coming back in.

He could have, true, but for some reason, perhaps it was a glance at who it was from, made him shove it hastily into his pocket. It wasn't until just now, hours later, when he reached into his pocket for his handkerchief that he felt it, and remembered the shock of seeing it.

Levi reached for the letter and frowned at it. As his eyes traced each letter of the sender's name, he knew one thing for sure. He didn't want to open it, even though he knew he had to. Taking a deep breath, he loosened the seal on the envelope.

A sudden set of footsteps made him look up. A young woman was with one of the horses, slipping a lead around its nose. He hadn't realized he wasn't alone. Hurriedly, he shoved the letter back into his pocket.

Levi wasn't sure why he said what he did, but with a few quick steps, he stopped in front of her, arms crossed, and asked, "Do you know what they do to horse thieves?"

It just burst out, even though he then recognized the horse thief was none other than his boss's daughter. He'd never met her personally before, though he'd seen her from a distance. The shock on her face, that quickly turned to embarrassment and then indignation made him fight to hide his smile.

"This is my horse," she answered stiffly. "And who are you?"

Levi uncrossed his arms. "Name's Levi Patterson. Your father hired me to help train some of his horses."

Rose nodded, her hand still on the horse's lead. "I see. Well then, maybe that's what you should go and do, and leave me alone, Mr. Patterson."

Someone was in a bad mood. He wondered why, as he glanced up at the large home. The Aldens were one of the wealthiest families around, with Mr. Alden's father having struck gold out in California decades before. There was nothing that family wanted for, and it appeared to him that their daughter was pretty spoiled herself. He recalled what Jim had said the night before, about her having gumption, and he couldn't help but agree. She had a lot of it.

Perhaps a little too much. Maybe that's why she couldn't get married off. No man liked a woman with a sharp tongue. Wit was fine. You wanted someone smart—at least he did—but a sweet nature was preferred, in his books. Still, her being married or not wasn't any of his business anyway. He'd known the Aldens thought highly of themselves. She seemed to be continuing that trend. He'd asked around before accepting the job of wrangler.

In town, the family had a reputation for keeping to themselves, and not mingling with most of the folk. That was part of the reason he wanted to work here. That, and their large ranch was well beyond the town's outskirts. Secluded.

With a shrug, wordlessly he turned, dusting himself off, and got a bucket of feed to make sure the few empty stalls remaining were filled with fresh food and water. The stable boy would be returning with the horses that were out to pasture, as it would be dark in about an hour. Which made him wonder why Miss Alden wanted to go out riding so late. It wasn't any of his business though, Levi reminded himself. He was here to work, take care of the horses, and keep his head low.

Especially the last part.

This was a good job, and not one that he wanted to risk losing because he made a mistake and his family found him.

Levi could sense her still staring at him, until she gasped and pulled her horse's lead, returning Ruby to her stall hastily.

Curiously, he watched as she ducked down, a panicked expression on her face.

Chapter 3

"Patterson! Have you seen my daughter?"

Rose narrowed her eyes and held her breath. Would the ranch hand tell her father she was with Ruby? She didn't doubt it, a man like that. While she might not know him, she knew his type. Eager to please her father and keep his job. Not many men paid as well as he did. It was a privilege to work for him.

Or so he often told everyone. Her father said a lot of things. A sense of humility wasn't something that he had.

"No, sir," the answer came from the wrangler.

She blinked in surprise. The man hadn't said anything. Why? There was no time to figure it out though. Her father's voice came closer and her muscles clenched in fear.

"How's the mare?" he asked. Rose could hardly breathe. She closed her eyes. He was just a few steps away. If he saw her, what would he say? Her parents had told her to spend less time with horses, and here she was, not just with her horse but crouched down in the straw and muck. How would she explain that?

"I expect she will birth in the next two weeks," the wrangler said.

His voice was pleasing to her ear, and she might have enjoyed listening to him talk, if she hadn't been so irritated with him, and worried about getting caught.

The man continued, "She made the trip just fine. We stopped as she needed, but she's strong, and I expect the foal to be as well."

"Send for me right away, night or day," her father commanded. "I want to be there to see it. I already have a buyer." And then she heard his footsteps fade.

It was just like him. His horses meant more than anything else. Except for his reputation. And his money. Those were of the most importance, and why he insisted that she marry someone both well off and who was in a position of power to increase her family's own. It wasn't enough to be well off, her father had told her before. It was important to be powerful too.

But at what cost? Certainly not one that he would ever pay. As a man, he could do whatever he wanted. But women? They had little control over things, and it wasn't fair. She was more than capable of doing anything she wanted.

And what she wanted was something she'd likely never have. It wasn't just freedom to be herself. It was a chance of freedom for making a living too. Rose didn't want to belong to a rich man, sitting in her house, gardening, or checking the servants weren't taking the silverware.

No, she wanted a business of her own, like her father had. A way to feel needed and accomplished. A part of something bigger than herself.

She'd watched him since she was a child. He had a sharp mind, one that she also possessed. There was something thrilling about the idea of starting something from nothing. Finding a need that needed filling and doing it. Working hard to grow it, cultivate it, eventually hire more people to expand it.

Rose wasn't sure what kind of business she wanted, just that she wanted one, and with her skills at using a needle—well, let's just say sewing and baking, two of the womanly businesses deemed acceptable to most, were out of the picture.

While she was fuming, and wondering if it was safe to stand and come out, the wrangler's head appeared over the stable door.

"He's gone," he said. "But you'd best hurry back."

Rose stood, her face flaming as she hastily brushed bits of straw off herself. He opened the stable door and she slipped out. Pausing, she looked over her shoulder. "Thank you, Mr. Patterson," she said. There was more she wanted to say; the words "thank you" seemed insignificant, but anything she might have told him seemed to catch in her throat.

She wasn't sure why that was. Fear of her father returning? Her haste to leave the barn? The warm eyes of the wrangler? His smile that no longer seemed mocking, but understanding? Rose couldn't think about that now. She had to hurry back.

Rose left the barn and took a last look over her shoulder to see him still watching her. Heedless of his gaze, she ran toward the house, her skirts held high enough so she wouldn't trip on them.

***

At dinner, her mother dominated the conversation, talking endlessly about Douglas West. His wealth. His family. How much land they owned. How many cattle. How many horses. His uncle was a politician. Another uncle a successful businessman back East. His father a rich banker. Rose stifled her yawns and nodded politely. Soon, she felt as though her head might wobble off, it had bobbed so much.

"And you'll be on your best behavior," her father said gruffly. "We don't have many opportunities in a place such as this to wed you off to a man of our station or higher, and you've ruined the last few chances. You'll behave tomorrow night, talking only when spoken to."

"Unless it's to flatter him," her mother added, leaning forward to be sure Rose saw her. "And not in that sarcastic way you tend to do."

Rose wanted to argue. But she couldn't. Her father was right on all accounts. Yes, they did have few chances to meet those in the same position as they were, and yes, she had ruined her father's chances at her successful marriage the last three times a man had shown her interest.

The first, she'd flat out told him she wasn't interested in being wed, and then the next hadn't liked she was cleverer than he was, and the most recent, she'd beaten him in a horse race. Oh, he'd tried to make it as though he let her win, but as a fine horsewoman, she'd easily and quickly outpaced him, then made the mistake of telling him how he held his reins incorrectly. The man's ego couldn't take that.

Her mother couldn't be any more obvious about this newest man, but the thinly veiled threats she wove throughout the meal, of what would happen if Rose didn't cooperate this time, did make her a little nervous.

"Your sisters did their duty," her mother intoned. "It's well past time you married, cemented yourself into another family, and helped grow the expanse of our family's influence."

It was difficult to eat the flaky savory pastry before her, stuffed with wild herbs and vegetables, and usually her favorite thing their cook made. Her nerves were all jangled up into a small ball and bouncing around inside her stomach.

The end of dinner couldn't, and didn't, come too soon for Rose. She withdrew to her room on the pretense of a headache and stood there moments later, staring through her window. For miles around, green pastures, a few animals, and homes and buildings dotted the landscape.

They had been living here her entire life. As she grew older, she often wondered what it would be like to live in one of those houses. Smaller than hers, likely with far less wealth, but perhaps without the expectations and pressures placed upon her. It seemed to her, in other families a person was allowed to marry out of love or desire, not just to further one's successes.

Of course, that would never be her. It hadn't been for her sisters either, though they hadn't seemed to mind one bit. Idly, she wondered what it would be like to run away, to live by herself doing whatever she wanted. She could dress how she liked, only eat the foods she enjoyed, and never worry about approval over what she wanted to read. The idea wasn't unappealing. It would be a fair trade, giving up most of her dresses and even someone to cook meals if she could just have the freedom to do what she wanted, like everyone else could.

As she dressed for bed, Rose very seriously considered the possibility. She was resourceful and determined. Her life wouldn't be ordinary, and she'd marry a man she loved. She'd have it no other way.

Even if she had to take matters into her own hands.

Chapter 4

Once alone, Levi pulled the letter out from his pocket once more. After making sure no one was around to interrupt him this time, he opened it, scanned the contents quickly, and then with a grimace read at a proper speed.

An ache spread in his chest, and his whole body felt tense. He realized that he was squeezing the letter when he tried to read it for a third time and couldn't make out some of the words. Slowly, being almost overly careful, Levi folded the letter with a frown. He tucked it back into the envelope as he weighed his options.

How had they found him? He'd been so careful. The news was unwelcome—both in that his secret wasn't entirely safe anymore, and that his father was unwell.

It left him with a hard choice. But for now, he didn't plan to answer. In fact, if he could convince himself to burn the letter or to pretend he'd never gotten it, he would. Not because he was an uncaring son, but because of what the letter meant. He'd have to go back.

As he continued about his chores then checked on the pregnant mare, his mind had trouble focusing. Frustrated with himself, he went out to the pasture where a half dozen new horses grazed. He felt pride knowing he'd ridden out with a few of the ranch hands working for Mr. Alden to bring his new horses home.

Now, he got the enjoyment of training them. Two had never had a saddle on their backs, and he knew it was going to take time. But that was okay. It was something he enjoyed doing, and something that he'd have never had an opportunity to do if he was back home.

No, Levi reflected, as he scrubbed his hands through his short cropped blonde curls, if he was back home, he'd be under his family's thumb. Married who they wanted. Be working where they wanted. He'd be smiling on the outside and screaming on the inside. Trapped in a cage created of expectations and demands.

His sister knew what that felt like. Megan was smart. Incredibly sharp, and she had both an instinct and a desire to learn. Medicine was what interested her, but as a woman, she knew she wouldn't have the chance. Their parents wouldn't allow it.

Once she married, she had little time and even less ability to learn more about the world she desired to know. He'd watched her, and realized that even though he was a man, with supposedly more opportunities, back home there weren't any for him.

It's why he left. Well, part of it, anyway. And why he didn't want to go back. Which drew his mind back to the letter. It had been on his bunk when he'd returned. He'd asked, but the stable boy only said that someone had ridden up, he didn't know who, and asked the wrangler be given it.

Levi started to pace. What if the letter was false? Maybe his father wasn't unwell. It also could be this was a ruse. A joke, even. He didn't even know how bad off he was. As he worried the questions circling in his mind, he wondered how he could he find out.

Perhaps his sister would know. He could write her and she'd keep his secret. She promised to always keep his secrets. But who was it who had found him? He had thought he was hundreds of miles away from anyone who might, and it had been at least four years since he'd left home.

Closing his eyes for a moment, he replayed his every action since arriving here, sure he'd done nothing to give himself away. He couldn't figure it out, yet someone obviously knew who he was and how to find him. The thought made him feel more than a little sick to his stomach.

Levi took a deep breath and steadied himself as he moved toward one of the horses. He needed to calm down. They'd sense his increased heartrate, his frustration, and it would make them skittish. That could lead to an injury, his or theirs. An injury would mean no job.

Patiently, he tried to clear his mind. To think of something else. But to his surprise, what popped into it was the image of a spirited dark-haired woman, her hair long and flowing in the breeze, her cheeks pink, and a haughty expression on her beautiful face as she stood before him with her arms crossed.

Why in the world was he suddenly thinking about Rose Alden? It made him feel both guilty and disloyal at once.

Chapter 5

Rose kept her eyes fixed on her plate. Mr. West had sent an apology that he couldn't dine with them, and between her mother's dramatics and her father's glaring at her, she wished she could turn into one of the flies buzzing around the room and leave.

"I hope he didn't hear talk about you," her father grumbled as he stabbed at his roasted chicken. "A girl like you isn't easy to marry off."

"And you looked so pretty tonight," her mother sighed. "I really thought we'd have a chance this time."

"Especially if you kept your mouth shut," her father agreed, and let out a grunt of disapproval. He shared a look with his wife, and at her nod they both stared at Rose in a way which made her feel quite uncomfortable and more than a little nervous. Speaking again, he said, "Rose, we have done you a disservice. I think the time has come."

"The time for what?" Rose asked, her voice faint. Beneath the table, her legs began to shake in worry.

Her parents traded another look, and her mother spoke then. "We have written to your aunt Rosemary in California, asking if we can send you to her. In the past, she offered to find you a suitable young man to marry. I'm sure it will be no different now."

Rose shot up in her chair. "But why? Why her?" It didn't matter that she'd been named after her aunt—Rose, short for Rosemary—the woman bore no resemblance to her in any way whatsoever. In fact, the limited interactions Rose had with her aunt had not been the least bit enjoyable.

"Why? Because, you need to do right by your family and make a successful match. In another year, you'll be a spinster. You'll never find anyone who will want you then. Your wealth is an advantage, Rose, but your ways are not. Though we have tried, it seems that we have failed. Your aunt, perhaps, will not," her father said, in the tone of voice that brooked no argument. "Your mother has written to her this afternoon, and we will be sure to have a reply soon."

Sucking in a sharp breath, Rose fought every instinct within her to bolt from the table. That wouldn't help her cause at all. It would only further justify her parents' criticism that she was impulsive and didn't care about appearances. It didn't matter they had no guests; someone was always watching, her mother warned her. Especially with as much help as they had hired.

So, Rose lowered her head, bit her lip, and squeezed her hands together tightly in her lap. She counted slowly to herself, trying to calm her breathing and the hot flashes of anger that filled her.

Once she was sure she had control of herself, she answered, "Whatever you say, Father. Mother."

Her parents resumed their conversation as though nothing had been said, and she was ignored for the rest of the meal. That was fine by her. She didn't even have to pretend the headache that crept into her temples.

Once alone in her room, Rose threw herself on her bed and let hot tears fall. Going to live with her aunt would be even worse than staying here. Her aunt lived in a town, in a small house close to many people. There would be no freedom at all for her. She knew this from the visits she'd had there. Her aunt didn't allow her to stay in her room. If she wished to read, it must be in her view. She wasn't allowed to ride horses, to go for a walk alone, or even to have tea in her room. Everything must be done under her aunt's watchful eye. In fact, Rose was quite sure her aunt had checked on her multiple times throughout the night to be sure she was sleeping. The woman had no trust in her whatsoever.

An absolute busybody, her aunt knew everyone and everything about them. Why, to her mother, she might be a wealth of knowledge, but the very idea of someone knowing so much about another made Rose shudder. Her aunt had shown her a book once. Inside of it, she had a page about each person that she knew or knew of. It listed acquaintances, scandals, and occupations. Her aunt took meddling to an entirely different level than most.

And it made her wonder just what sort of information her aunt had on her, and who she planned to pair her with. It was all done in an exacting way, and all based off her many notes.

She knew how to wed people. Excelled at it. It seemed her unusual way of matching people worked well. Her own daughters had married successfully. Each was married to a man with wealth, an impressive reputation, or power. Married happily? That was a different story. Her daughters' hopes and pleas weren't taken into consideration at all, so Rose had no doubt in her mind that hers would be ignored as well.

She rolled over suddenly and sat up. Perhaps she'd been going about this all wrong. What if what she needed wasn't a forced marriage, but to find one that her parents would be pleased with, though it was a man she chose?

The idea was exciting. Should she approach her mother with it? Surely her mother would listen to her. She'd been young once. Had loved, once.

Just as soon as the hope bloomed, it was crushed. Her parents had washed their hands of her. Her only hope now was in an aunt who was unlikely to see reason at her reluctance to be married to the first suitable man.

Time was running out, and so were her chances to make her own way. She just needed to figure out what that was.

Chapter 6

Levi took off his hat as he walked into the post office, and the woman behind the window looked up at him and smiled. "Can I help you?" she asked.

"I'd like to post this, please," he said, handing over the slightly crumpled letter.

For several days, he'd worried over the letter he'd gotten. Finally, he had written to his sister. Was it true his father was on his deathbed? Against his better wishes, he'd told her she could reply here. He didn't know how the original letter had found him, but perhaps traveling a town over and using their post office, and their return address, he would keep himself a little safer, a little less visible.

Walking out of the post office, he spotted someone who seemed vaguely familiar. He stopped and squinted. It almost looked like the person who'd pushed past him the night he returned to the ranch with the horses.

Was he being followed?

Levi tried not to let the person see he noticed them, and went into the general store. When he peered through the window, on the pretense of looking at something, the person was gone. Irritation filled him, and then practicality. Might as well grab a few things while he was here. He chose a new shirt, some shaving soap, and a new razor, then looked over their boots. He'd be needing a new pair soon, and they had a bigger selection than he'd seen anywhere else.

Paying for his purchases, he went back, secured them into his saddlebags, and mounted his horse. The ride back to the Alden ranch didn't seem to take long, and he checked frequently, but no one else was nearby, so it must have been a coincidence that the person he'd seen resembled the unknown hand on the Alden ranch.

It was hot and dry today. In fact, Levi couldn't remember the last time it rained. The creeks were low, if not empty, and everything, himself included, seemed to be wilting. What they needed was a good soaking. That would damp down the dirt, fill the wells, and keep the gardens alive.

As he approached the ranch, thick dust from his horse's hooves clouding the air, Levi spotted a woman near the barn. He rode closer and saw it was Rose Alden. She looked up as he approached.

For some reason, his stomach felt strange when he saw her. He hadn't ever felt a flutter like that before. Must have been that sandwich from the diner, he guessed, nothing more. That cheese had tasted a little moldy though it had looked fine. That must be it.

He swung down from his horse. "Hello," he said.

She nodded, looked down, and then back at him with a look on her face he couldn't decipher. "Hello," she answered, and then looked away again.

Then it hit him. He'd seen that look before. His sister had worn it many times just before she was married. He squinted at her for a moment. Rose's eyes were red, her face looked blotchy, and she was decidedly quiet. That wasn't what he'd expected from her, not after their first meeting.

"Need some help? I'm happy to saddle Ruby for you, if you want to ride out a while," he said. It was best not to mention anything about her looking upset. He knew without a doubt she wouldn't care for that.

She froze, almost stiffly, then nodded. "Please."

He worked quickly, grabbing a saddle and buckling it onto her horse. As he slipped the bit into the horse's mouth and made sure the reins were connected securely, he stole another look at her.

Rose was staring at the pasture beyond the barn. There was a small wooded area that was shaded right now. A short distance from it was a small creek that wound its way through the Alden property and, if followed long enough, would lead to town in one direction. He'd not examined it but once, but he imagined it would be the perfect place for leisure. Perhaps a packed lunch and a book, or even a nap. Was that what Rose had intended? A peaceful respite?

"Here you are," Levi said.

She looked distracted. And upset. Her long dark hair was loose, and a breeze lifted it, waving it gently. She turned then, and took the reins he held out silently.

"Thank you," she said. Her fingers brushed his as she accepted the reins, and a spark of electricity burned in his fingertips. Levi nearly jolted. What had that been? He couldn't tell if she noticed anything. She led Ruby to the mounting block.

"Want me to hold her?" Levi offered.

"I can do it," Rose said. Then, in a bitter tone, added, "I won't have much longer with her, so I want to do all I can while I still can."

She mounted quickly, and before he could puzzle more over her comment, rode out of the barn with Ruby in a fast walk.

Levi turned, checking on the pregnant mare, and then took one of Mr. Alden's new horses from the stall to work on training it. He let himself get lost in the moment, in part because he had to stay focused on the horse for safety, and part because he relished each moment. Training horses, caring for horses, teaching others about horses—it was his passion. If he never could do another thing in his lifetime, he'd be just fine with that.

Did he feel lonely at times? Levi supposed he did. He missed his family some days. And he knew that being on the run, he'd never have the opportunity to find a woman and settle. It would require telling her the truth, something that he would do because he couldn't stand lies. But what woman would want to be with him, knowing what she could have had?

Carol had been willing. But as soon as her parents and his had learned she was wanting to run away with him after a quick wedding, she'd been married off so fast he was still blinking. Now, she was another man's wife, and the woman he thought he loved didn't complain one single bit.

Why would she? It was just one more instance of a woman wanting him for what she thought he could offer, not who he was.

The thought made Levi feel a bitter taste in his mouth. He didn't regret giving up what he had, but there was a worry that kept surfacing after the mysterious letter.

What if he was forced to go back home? What then?

Chapter 7

Rose watched the wrangler. He couldn't see her from her position in the trees, but as Ruby nibbled on the grass and drank her fill from the barely trickling creek, she could watch him.

At first, the wrangler looked content. Focused. Enjoying each moment with the new horse. But then his face grew concerned. Strained and tight. Almost as though there was a terrible thought he couldn't shake. For some reason that she couldn't quite understand, Rose felt sympathetic. He looked the way that she felt.

From her spot on the soft green grass, her horse nearby and a book in her lap, Rose let herself drift into a daydream. In this one, her aunt had found her the perfect man to marry. One who liked to have conversations that included her, not talked over her. Someone who enjoyed the same things she did. Perhaps, even someone who wasn't afraid to dirty his hands with the day-to-day chores.

It was silly though, for her to think that. No such man would be of a high enough position for her aunt or her parents to consider him marriage material.

With a heavy sigh, Rose looked out into the pasture again. The wrangler was gone, and so was the horse. A glance at the sky suddenly darkening told her she needed to go as well.

She'd hardly grabbed Ruby's harness when a crack of thunder sounded, startling both her and the horse. Deciding that leading Ruby would be safer, Rose tugged on the horse, urging her forward.

Rain fell then, pelting them, and Ruby finally moved. The barn seemed so far away, and the rain blinded Rose as she held one hand in front of her face, trying to find her way.

There was a bright flash of lighting in the now dusky sky, and another, louder, crack of thunder. Ruby reared up, ripping the reins from Rose and sending her tumbling backward under the raised horse's hooves.

She rolled to the side, getting out of the way just as Ruby landed and tried to run. Without thinking, Rose grabbed on to the dangling reins and, partially dragged, managed to get her footing and pulled on the horse. "Woah," she yelled, trying to be heard over the storm. "Woah."

Ruby wasn't listening. It was obvious she was scared. By now, the rain had filled the small creek, threatening to overflow. How had it happened so quickly? Between the water rushing, the rain beating on them, the lightning and the thunder, Rose was getting worried.

She pulled Ruby toward the direction she thought the barn was, only to feel a sudden sense of panic. When the horse had bolted, they'd gotten turned around. She knew her horse had a good sense of direction, but the rain was pelting them, and the screaming of the wind was alarming Ruby. She became skittish, pulling in a direction that Rose wasn't sure was the right one.

Should she trust her horse to lead her home? Or was that a mistake? Rose wasn't sure where they were. She just knew the storm had turned deadly, and she was scared.

Chapter 8

Levi stood at the barn looking out at the storm. It had been a while since he'd seen one this bad. He couldn't even make out the small crop of trees he knew was in the distance. He turned, rubbing at a shoulder. The new horse had given him a workout. He was glad for the storm, it meant he could rest a while.

He passed the stalls and checked on each horse. The thunder was making them restless. He came to the last stall and then froze. It was empty. He quickly ran through the horses' names, and realized Ruby was missing. The last he'd seen, Rose was with her. That meant they were both out in the storm.

He didn't think twice. Levi grabbed a thick blanket, a lead rope, and ran to the last place he'd seen Rose. She had been heading to the creek. It wasn't really too far away, but if she wasn't back yet, something must have happened, either to her or to the horse. He had to find her. Even if she'd managed to find shelter, he couldn't leave her alone. The horses were in his care, and he was responsible for them.

Levi tried to ignore the worry that formed from the thought Rose might be hurt, as well. It wasn't just his job he was concerned about, but the spirited woman. Standing in the pouring rain, he felt an overwhelming sense of concern for her.

He pushed through the strong wind and rain that soaked him instantly. Moving in a straight line, he headed toward the creek and hoped he'd find it, and Rose. He wasn't very familiar with the area. In the distance he thought he heard something, and froze, his ears straining against the sounds of the storm surrounding him.

When he didn't hear whatever it was again, he pushed forward once more. A moment later, he heard the sound again.

Levi moved as quickly as he could, and then he saw them. Rose, pushing as hard as she could on Ruby, who wouldn't budge. He ran up to her. Rose was soaking wet, her long hair dripping with rain, and she met his eyes, looking both panicked and surprised. He wrapped the blanket around her, and took Ruby's reins.

The horse went easily for him, only giving a little resistance, nothing like she'd done with Rose. "Stay close," he called.

There was a cracking sound, and a large branch fell off a tree behind them, right where Rose had been standing but a moment before. Her eyes wide, she moved closer to him, and they started back to the barn.

Every step was a struggle. The wind pushed against them and small branches skittered in their path, but a short time later, they'd made it back to the safety of the barn.

Levi rubbed Ruby down once he got her into her stall. Rose sat shivering, and he looked around for another blanket, one that was dry. "We need to get you back to the house," he said.

"No, I can't go in like this," Rose said through chattering teeth.

"You also can't stay like this, you'll get sick," Levi argued.

"Good," she said. Her defiant glare surprised him. "Maybe then they won't send me away."

"Send you away?" Levi felt confused. He found another blanket and handed it to her. She wrapped it around herself and sighed as she snuggled into the warmth.

"Yes," Rose said. She frowned then, looking into the distance. "I'm a disappointment and a failure. So, I'm being sent away. Seeing me like this just gives them a reason to do it sooner."

Levi blinked. "Is that so?"

He knew that was weak. It wasn't a proper answer. He wished he had a hot drink to offer her. To have for himself. Then he remembered. The small stove in the barn and his saddlebag he'd dropped near it. "Wait a moment," he said. "Follow me."

In only a few minutes, he had water on to boil, and two beat up tin mugs sitting on a low stool. Rose watched silently from another stool. It wasn't long before Levi handed Rose one of the mugs, now filled with tea, and watched as she drank from it.

She moved closer toward the stove. "Thank you," she said. And then she added, "And thank you for coming to find me. I don't know what I'd have done if you hadn't. Ruby was quite scared."

"I'm just glad I checked the stalls once more before I headed to my bunk," Levi said. He drank deeply, letting the warm liquid spread through his stomach. It felt good, and he was finally starting to not feel chilled. The stove was drying his clothes, and he inched closer to the alluring heat, the same as Rose had.

"That storm came out of nowhere," Rose mused. "I've never seen anything like it."

Levi nodded in agreement. "It sure did. It's a good thing you weren't much further away. We only just made it back as it is." He took a moment to study her. The slump of her shoulders wasn't just because she was cold. He refilled her mug. "Sorry it's such a weak tea," he told her. "Don't keep a lot in the barn. This is just what happened to be in a saddlebag."

"It's just what I needed," she answered. She sighed then and looked over at Levi. "I'd drink this every day if it meant I got to make my own choices."

"You say that," Levi said, settling back more comfortably in his spot on the ground and letting his eyes take in the storm raging outside. It had shown no signs of slowing. "But when it actually happens, it's a shock. Not everyone can adjust."

"I could," Rose said, straightening her back. Then, she turned to him with a curious expression. "What would you know about it, anyway?"

Levi wished he hadn't said anything. For a moment, he felt so comfortable sitting here with Rose. She felt easy to talk to and it had slipped out. His mind spun and he wondered how to recover the situation. "Just what I imagine. What I hear," he said, but even to himself, it didn't sound convincing.

She crossed her arms and fixed him with that look he'd gotten used to very quickly. The one that was part haughty, part disbelief. "Is that so?" she asked. Then she raised her eyebrows. "You aren't telling me something."

He laughed then. "Since when does the help tell their whole life's story to the bosses' daughter?"

"So, there *is* a story," she exclaimed triumphantly, and leaned in closer. Her finger pointed at him. "Tell me. Unless you are a criminal." She sat back then, squinting at him. "Maybe that's why you don't want to tell me?"

Still feeling amused, he looked at her. Should he say anything more? He'd likely regret it later, but Levi studied her for a long moment. Then he answered. "Fine. But can I count on your secrecy?" he asked.

"Not if you are a criminal," she said, wrapping the blanket around her a little tighter.

"I'm not," he said. Then fixed her with his own look of disdain. "I'm disappointed you'd think that. If not about me, then about your father. You think he'd hire a criminal?"

"I'm sure he has at some point," she shrugged.

Her reply was so casual. So matter of fact. He'd think on that at a later time. But right then, Levi took a deep breath and a long drink of his tea.

"You can stall," Rose said, "but I'm going to wait." She motioned to the storm beyond. "I'm sure not going out in that again."

"Like to know it all, don't you?" Levi asked mildly.

"It's the only way to learn," she answered, surprising him. "I don't get out a lot," she added wryly. "Smart women aren't encouraged. And too many questions or the desire to have a mind and opinions of your own, including that of who you want to marry, tends to get a girl sent away."

"Is that what they are really going to do?" Levi asked. The surprise in his voice couldn't be contained. And he wasn't trying to stall, to avoid her question, but he was curious.

Rose's eyes flashed with anger, but he didn't miss the quiver in her voice as she answered tightly, "Yes."

They sat silently for another moment, the only sound around them the storm outside. The wind had lessened in its ferocity, but the rain still fell to the ground at the speed of bullets.

Levi glanced over, and his eyes locked with Rose's. There was something in them that pulled him to her. There was a feeling of connection he'd never felt with someone before. Maybe it was their similarities. Maybe it was the fact they'd just narrowly escaped danger. But whatever it was, before he knew what he was doing, he'd blurted out his entire story.

Chapter 9

Rose didn't miss the fact that Levi seemed reluctant to tell his story, but she'd told hers, and it seemed only fair. When he was still quiet, she decided to tell him so. Before she could open her mouth though, he was talking.

"I wasn't always a wrangler. I grew up around horses, but only in that they were in the city, hooked to the carriages we rode in. My family and I lived in town, in a rather nice area where most people owned country homes. It was there they'd have their own horses, but my family, though well off, didn't have a country home. Instead, when my parents wished to go to the countryside, we'd rent a home for a month."

Mr. Patterson darted a quick look at her and shrugged, "My father is a doctor. There's my older sister and me. The disappointment. So, you see, I know what it's like to be considered that."

"But wait," Rose said, wrinkling her nose as she tried to puzzle his words. "How is it the son of a doctor is a wrangler? I cannot believe that your father would accept that. It seems so wildly different."

"He didn't," the wrangler gave a snort, "I didn't ask for permission. I simply left."

"Left?" she gasped, and leaned forward. "How? Why? When?"

He held up a hand. "One question at a time." Then he gave her a small frown. "But maybe I shouldn't say anything. I don't want to give you any ideas."

Rose rolled her eyes. "You won't give me any ideas I've not had," she said. "However, I assure you, I won't be running away. Despite what others think, I do respect my parents' wishes."

The wrangler gave her a look then. It was an appraising one that she couldn't quite understand. Somehow, it made her cheeks warm and she quickly raised her mug to disguise her discomfort. Was it that his eyes were too piercing? They seemed to see right in her. Was it the fact that yes, perhaps he did understand. Or, was it that she'd never been alone and so close to a man before?

He didn't seem to notice her discomfort, and went back to his story. "I was expected to take up a profession, marry well, and further advance the family. My father being a doctor, it was thought perhaps I'd be the same. Yet, I had no interest in medicine. That belonged to my sister, who would read every one of our father's medical journals. She longed to assist him, but my father thought women had no place in medicine, and he and my mother insisted she marry, and marry well to improve our family's status."

"Sounds familiar," Rose muttered. "So, did she?"

He nodded. "She did. Reluctantly. She's married to a man who runs several banks."

"But what about you?" Rose pressed. "How did you end up here?"

He stood and refilled her mug, then his. Once he settled back near the stove, he said, "There was a woman. I thought I was in love with her. We planned to get married, run away together, leave the expectations of our parents behind." He frowned then, and his jaw clenched. "Her parents found out and forced her to marry someone else the same day to preserve her reputation. She didn't seem to mind at all. As for me and my father? We had an argument. My father sent me away. I was to go—" and then he stopped.

"Go on," Rose insisted.

"I don't want to give you ideas," he said, looking down at his boots.

"What do you mean?" she asked.

He looked away, to where the rain had lightened. Though it was still heavy, the wind had stopped pushing it sideways. Finally, he said, "I was sent away to my uncle. He's a lawyer, and my father said if I didn't want to be a doctor, I'd become a lawyer. I boarded the train and switched first chance I got."

Rose shook her head. "I don't understand. What do you mean?"

"I mean, I never went to my uncle. I took train after train until I ended up out West. Once there, I wrote to my parents so they wouldn't worry about me. I told them I was going to live my own life. I write letters now and again, never giving my address, but I am now making my own decisions. Not them."

"That's...incredible," Rose said. She was silent a moment. "That also must have taken a lot of courage."

"It's been hard at times, too," he admitted. "You know how it is. You grow up with servants. People who worry about all the details you don't even think about. Cooking, for one. Where to buy things. Making money and making sure it lasts for what you need. Though we were not as well off as your family, I still always had people to do the things I didn't want to do or know how to do. Being on my own was eye opening."

"So that's why you said what you did earlier," Rose said. "I guess you do know what it's like." She slumped then. She was torn between feeling envious, and feeling hopeless. When she'd told him that she wasn't going to imitate what he'd done, that she was obedient and respectful of her parents' wishes, she meant that.

But there was something else she wanted. If her time was limited before she would be wed to someone she had no say over, she at least wanted to do some choosing of things for herself.

And she knew the very first thing, but she couldn't tell him now.

"The rain is light enough I can go," Rose said. It was true. It had lightened to a steady but now relenting storm. "But I want to ask you something tomorrow. Can we meet? Perhaps go for a ride?"

The wrangler shrugged. "I don't see why not," he said. "After lunch?"

"Perhaps," Rose said, and smiled. She stood, and the blanket that had been wrapped around her pooled at her feet. She picked it up, folded it, and handed it to Mr. Patterson.

Once again, their fingers brushed and her breath caught. Yes. She knew exactly what she was going to ask him

Rose wanted him to be her first kiss.

Chapter 10

Swiping his sleeve across his forehead, Levi frowned as he looked through one of the barn windows. How had the incredible storm yesterday not broken the heat? On one hand, yes, the creek was filled now, but on the other, the storm had not only caused damage in the gardens and to the property, but it had also made it incredibly humid.

He strode to the water bucket and filled the ladle, drank deeply, and then refilled it, drinking once more. His ears strained, listening for the sound of Rose coming. He couldn't help it. Against his wishes, she clouded his mind all night, making him toss and turn.

What was it about her that had disturbed him? Was it worry or curiosity about what she wanted to talk to him about? Concern over her plight?

Levi wasn't entirely certain how he felt about her being sent away. After all, it wasn't an uncommon thing. Many family members in larger cities had nieces and nephews or grandchildren sent in by the dozens in hope of a potential spouse. It had likely always been that way, hoping that a successful match would be made. However, perhaps it was because he understood what it felt like to be the family disappointment that made him feel sympathetic.

And by default tired, as he'd not slept, the yawn he tried to stifle reminded him.

The crunch of boots on the small stones of the path to the barn pricked his ears, and he looked up. There was Rose, walking closer to the barn, the look on her face one could only ever describe as determination. No wonder she unsettled her parents. He hardly knew her and felt uncomfortable seeing her expression.

"Afternoon," Levi said, as she drew closer.

"Good afternoon," she replied, twisting her fingers around her skirt.

"I've got Ruby saddled for you," Levi said. "If you are still wanting to go for a ride?"

Rose nodded, and her dark hair swung into her face. As she pushed it back behind her ears, she said, "Yes. My parents will be gone all afternoon, so I can enjoy myself."

With a nod, Levi brought out Ruby, and then mounted his own horse, Buckeye. "Where to?" he asked.

"I'll show you," Rose said, and took the lead.

Buckeye followed Ruby, and the horses took them several minutes past the small gathering of trees he'd rescued Rose and Ruby at the night before. When the trees thinned and a wide field filled with wildflowers opened before them, Levi blinked several times to be sure it was real. From the corner of his eye, he saw Rose staring at him with a grin.

"Isn't it incredible?" She looked back out into the field. "It's almost like a secret, this place. Father doesn't ever use it, because it's a bit far from the line of sight of the barn for the horses. I love it though. Mother has her garden, it's all neat and tidy and perfect. But this...this is so wild. So messy. So free. That's what makes it perfect," Rose said with a happy sigh.

Something about that little sound made him shiver. Rose slipped off her horse then, and let Ruby wander over to a thick patch of grass. Levi also dismounted, and let Buckeye do the same.

They stood there in silence for a long moment until Rose turned to him. "Thank you," she said, "for sharing your story with me yesterday. For the first time ever, I felt understood."

He shrugged. But then he raised an eyebrow. "I am counting on your discretion," he reminded her.

"I promise," she said, and then her head tipped, and she looked at him. There was something she wanted to say, to ask. He could tell, but she didn't speak any further.

Levi watched as Rose walked to a large rock and sat, leaning her back against it. He joined her and they sat quietly. He felt like he should say something, so he decided to say the first thing that came to mind. "Miss Alden—"

"Rose," she corrected. "I want you to call me Rose."

He wasn't sure if it was fully proper, but he nodded. "Levi," he offered. At her smile, he continued, "Miss—Rose, when you go, I just want you to know that I'll be hoping for the best for you."

"I appreciate it," she answered. Then she turned to him with a serious expression. "I don't know how long it will be before my parents do send me away. It might only be days. In the meantime, I'm determined to make my own decisions as much as I can and do the things I want to do, just in case I never have the chance again."

"Makes sense," Levi agreed.

"Then, will you help me with one of them?" Rose asked.

"If I can," he answered. "What do you need?"

The corners of Rose's mouth turned up, and with her eyes fixed on his, she said, "I want you to be the first person to kiss me."

Chapter 11

His reaction was not what she expected. Levi's face turned white, then red, then a strange color she wasn't sure what. He sputtered, "I—you—you—I—"

She waited for a moment, then interrupted. "Yes. I want you to kiss me. It's quite alright if you don't know how or aren't experienced." Her tone was frank. "I'm not either, but I do figure this will be the only chance I have to choose for myself who will be the person I kiss, and for the first time." She studied him for a moment. "I thought you, of all people, would understand that."

"I do," Levi still sputtered, trying to regain his train of thought, "but, you can't be serious."

Rose chose not to be offended. She was under no illusion that she was a beauty, nor was she desirable. But she was a woman, wasn't she? And he was a single man. She fixed him with a cool gaze. "I'm quite serious."

His eyes searched hers for a moment. "Rose," he said slowly. "I work for your father. I'm also in hiding. If someone found out..."

He didn't finish, but Rose nodded slowly. She understood. Her request would put him in as much trouble as it might her. So, she sighed. "Nevermind. It was just a thought."

When he opened his mouth, she put a finger against it. "Don't. I don't want your pity. I also don't want any lies from you." She took a deep breath, trying to hide the anger that started to bubble deep in her. "When I'm with my aunt, I'm sure I'll hear plenty of them."

"Like what?" His question was serious. Rose could see it in his eyes.

She scoffed, tossing her hair, "Like how beautiful I am. How fascinating. How wonderful. Really, those lies are hiding what others want to say. How rich I am. How well connected. How eligible." There was hurt in her words that had escaped from her heart, and she wondered if he could tell. Did he hear it?

To her horror, her lower lip began to tremble, and she focused on a single flower, trying to hold her tears in.

"There's always going to be that person," he told her then. "I heard plenty of that myself. Could see right through them as well."

Rose glanced at him, then away again. "Hurtful, isn't it?"

She could feel him settling into a more comfortable position next to her. "It's more...irritating," he said. "At least for me. I want someone to like me for myself. Not what I, or a family member, can do for them. Beyond giving love, I mean."

"Mmm." Rose let a finger trail over the tiny yellow flower. It was so delicate, she wondered how it had survived the storm. But, somehow, the fact that it had made her think that she, too, could survive when she left. Really, she had no choice, and she'd never admit to anyone, no one at all, if she wasn't happy. She'd never give that satisfaction.

"You're wrong about one thing, though," Levi said.

When she looked at him, he was staring right at her. "What?" she asked.

"Not everyone who says you are beautiful is going to be lying," he told her.

Rose rolled her eyes and snorted. It wasn't very ladylike, but neither was she, and she didn't care. She didn't need to be proper around the wrangler. That, in part, was why she enjoyed her time with him yesterday during the storm. She got to be herself.

"I mean it," he insisted.

Before Rose knew what was happening, he had leaned in closer, and his face was inches from hers.

"I think you are beautiful." His voice was low. "You've been on my mind all day, and I couldn't wait to see you again."

Rose lowered her eyes beneath her lashes. As her chin ducked slightly, a slightly calloused finger raised it up again. She didn't even have time to think before a set of warm lips pressed against hers, and the world seemed to spin.

Chapter 12

Levi let the kiss linger, then pulled back slowly. He wasn't sure why he'd done it. He had told himself he wouldn't. But as he'd looked at her, he couldn't seem to stop himself from moving closer and capturing her mouth.

He hadn't kissed anyone since Carol. And then, only her because he thought she was the one. As a familiar ache formed in his heart, threatening to distract him from this moment with Rose, he forced it to stop.

Carol was the past. Rose was right here in front of him. Beautiful, spirited, surprising.

Rose was blinking rapidly, and she brought her fingertips to her lips. She stared at him in surprise. Feeling embarrassed, he looked down. His cheeks had an unwelcome warmth to them. What now? He'd likely done something stupid. Very stupid.

A gentle touch on his arm caused him to raise his head. Rose was just as pink in the cheeks as he felt, but she was smiling. She didn't say anything, but moved a little closer to him and sat in silence. Her fingers crept near his, and rested, just barely touching him. After a moment, his body relaxed, and though they didn't say another word for the next half hour, he felt comfortable in a way like he'd never felt before. If he stayed this way forever, he'd be content.

Levi watched the horses grazing and in the warm sun found himself getting drowsy. Just as he thought he might drift off, Rose sighed. "I guess we'd better get back," she said reluctantly.

He nodded and stood, then offered a hand to her. She took it with a smile as he pulled her up.

They rode back to the barn, and Rose started to groom Ruby once she had her in the stall.

"I can do that," Levi offered, but she shook her head.

"No, it's my horse," she said.

They worked in quiet, and Levi took a moment to check on the pregnant mare. He'd just stepped back when Mr. Alden walked in. "How's she looking?" he asked.

Levi startled slightly. He hadn't heard the other man approaching until he spoke. "She's in good shape," he said. "Any day now."

His boss nodded, and then his gaze fell on his daughter. "Come in the house, Rose," he said. "Your mother and I want to speak with you. We've had a letter."

"May I finish grooming Ruby?" Rose asked.

Her father hesitated, then shook his head. "I don't think your mother wants to wait," he told her.

Rose lowered her head and nodded. Levi reassured her, "I'll finish for you."

She gave him a grateful look and slipped from the stall. Her father took several steps toward the barn door, and then stopped, looking over his shoulder. "Are you coming?" he asked.

"Yes, Father," Rose said, walking toward him. When her father's long legs carried him quickly to the path, Rose stopped, turned, and whispered, "At least I got to have one kiss I chose." A tear trickled down her cheek and Levi wanted nothing more than to wipe it away. Helpless, he watched as she squared her shoulders and walked briskly to catch up to her father, facing whatever it was about to come to her head on.

***

The next few days passed quickly. Levi worked hours at a time training the new horses, and then headed back to his bunk for a few moments of rest before dinner. He hadn't seen Rose and wondered, worried even, how she was.

She was on his mind as he entered the bunkhouse, again nearly being shoved by that unfamiliar ranch hand who was pushing past him. He looked up, irritation starting to fill him, when he froze. Once again, on his bed was an envelope. How had a reply gotten here so soon? His parents were not even in the same state. Did the mail really move that quickly? And why had it not gone to the post office?

His mouth went suddenly dry and he hesitated, scared to open the envelope. Taking a deep breath, he slid a finger under the seal and pulled out the single sheet inside. A small, feminine handwriting greeted him, and Levi sank onto his bunk and read it.

Dearest brother,

I hope this letter finds you well. Yes, it is true. Father is quite ill, and the doctor urges you to come in case these are his final days. I confess, I did not realize until your letter arrived that you did not know. He took ill some months ago, and though he insists he is recovering, the doctor seems to think otherwise.

Father and Mother were most distressed when you left those years ago. You are still their child and they love you dearly, even if the path you are on isn't what they'd have chosen for you. In fact, dare I say it, because they might not, they are proud of you.

However, the mystery of how the letter found you is because our parents have always known where you are and what you do. Once you were missing, they sent a private investigator to track you down, and report to them of your whereabouts.

While I do not know all of the particulars, it is how they choose to both let you have your freedom, and give themselves peace of mind.

With that said, won't you please write more often? It gives us all the greatest of pleasure and the most welcome relief to hear from you, and how I long to hear of your adventures. Father does as well.

Please, do not be cross with them, or with me. Come home, let the past be the past, and let us see you again, even if it's only for a while. We miss you so.

Your affectionate sister,

Marie

Levi closed his eyes. This whole time, they'd known? But then his sister's words came back to him, and he reread the lines. *You are still their child and they love you dearly, even if the path you are on isn't what they'd have chosen for you. In fact, dare I say it, because they might not, they are proud of you.*

He shook his head slowly. There was a feeling of betrayal. They had him watched! Did they not trust him to take care of himself? What were they worried about? Him as a person or his father's heir? Then his eyes fell on another line. *They choose to both let you have your freedom, and give themselves peace of mind.*

A pricking sensation formed in Levi's eyes. For years, he'd felt unloved. He had distanced himself because of his differences with his father, but perhaps the years had softened his father's heart?

More importantly, perhaps it had softened his. Levi put the letter in his pocket and set out in search of Jim to get him an audience with Mr. Alden. Maybe it was time to go home for a short visit. He just needed to get permission first.

Chapter 13

Rose refused to show her fear or her sorrow as the last of her trunks was packed. She glanced around her room, and through the window caught sight of her mother directing one of the ranch hands where to put her cases in the carriage.

Soon, she'd be leaving. When she returned—if she returned—it would be as a married woman. Her parents had made that abundantly clear.

There had been no time permitted to let her go to the stable and visit Ruby or Levi. Once, she'd slipped out for a moment, but he wasn't there and she left, disappointed, hurrying back to the house before her parents knew she was gone.

Though she'd hoped to see him, a small part of her was glad he wasn't there. What would she have said? I'll miss you? Thank you for the kiss? How are you? Rose couldn't believe that she, who never had trouble speaking her mind before, now suddenly didn't know what to say. That didn't stop her from wanting to *see* him, though.

A familiar pricking in her eyes appeared, and she blinked rapidly. No, she wouldn't give in to sorrow. Deep within, Rose knew this would be her fate. She'd always known it. Her life wasn't truly her own, no matter how much she wished it or had pretended that it was.

Childhood was over. It was time for her to become a woman. And without any say in the matter. She could delay it no longer.

Rose could hear her father's shout from downstairs. "Rose! Are you ready? The train won't wait, not even for us."

She sighed. "Coming, Father," she called, and snatched up the book she wanted to take with her.

"If you've forgotten anything," her mother said on the carriage ride to town, "just send me a message. If it's something of inconsequence, I'm sure your aunt will guide you to a store to purchase a new one. You are not, however, to take advantage of her generosity."

"Yes, Mother," Rose said quietly, as she watched from the small window as her home grew further and further away, and the town too swiftly appeared.

They pulled into the train station, and two of the ranch hands swiftly unloaded her bags, seeing they were taken on the train.

"Your aunt will have her men help with your baggage," her mother said, straightening the neck of Rose's travel dress. She fussed about for a moment until she stepped back and nodded, a pleased expression on her face. "Be sure to write once you are there."

Her father handed her an envelope. "Some cash for incidentals," he said. "Keep it safe."

Rose nodded and put it inside of her purse. She was still in disbelief she was going. And alone. The fact her parents weren't sending someone with her was a surprise.

"I'll miss you, dear," her mother said, "but isn't this exciting? My little girl, about to find herself a husband."

Every muscle in her body seemed to clench just then, and Rose fought back an urge to be sick. She knew it was the way, understood it even, that women had no say and no rights. However, it certainly didn't mean that she liked it, nor did she have to.

It was all too likely that her aunt had a half dozen young men lined up to parade her past. Snobby, horrid, chauvinist men. Ones who only wanted someone pretty to look at and keep their mouth shut. Weren't they in for a disappointment on both accounts!

A thought flickered in her mind, and though it was small, it was a powerful one. Perhaps when visiting her aunt, who lived in a larger town than Rose's family did, there would be others of the same opinions of her. Could it even be that such a thing might even be more widely accepted? Rose had heard that before—even read it once in a news article—but until this moment, she'd not even dared hope it could be an option for her.

Maybe leaving, as unwanted and unwelcome as it was, would be the start of something new. Something better.

Besides, just because she met men, didn't mean she'd have to marry one if she didn't want. She had her ways. She'd use them if she had to delay the inevitable for as long as possible.

Because if she was being truthful, the one thing Rose prided herself upon was that eventually, she would be married, by force or otherwise, and the sooner, in her parents' mind, the better.

"Rose," her father said. He cleared his throat. "You may not agree with our decision, but I promise you, it is not done out of punishment, but because it is what we feel is best for you."

"Better board now, miss," the stationmaster said as he walked up to her. "Train's leaving."

Rose nodded briskly. "Right. Well, then," she said, and fixed her mother with a serious look. "Take care, Mother, Father. I'm sorry I've been such an unwelcome disappointment. Perhaps Aunt Rosemary can remedy that."

Her mother gasped, and Rose sensed her father stiffen, but she didn't turn back as she angrily strode toward the train.

Hope of a better place or not, she was still very upset, and the hurt she knew she caused at her words was also the truth—and it hurt her even more to once again acknowledge it. More so than she was betting it hurt her parents to hear.

Rose slipped into her seat, and pointedly didn't look out the window until the train had well left the station.

If this was to be her new start in life, and perhaps even her final days as an unmarried woman, she would do things her way.

Chapter 14

"You wanted to see me?"

Levi turned, and then set down the saddle he had hoisted up only a moment before. "Yes, sir," he said. "If you have a moment, Mr. Alden."

The man nodded, and then peered at the mare. "What do you think?"

"Within a day. Maybe two," Levi said, and pushed up his hat. "Not much longer now, and I'm all ready."

"Good. That foal will be quite valuable. Already have a buyer."

Levi nodded.

Mr. Alden's gaze fixed on him then. "Jim said it was important. What did you need to talk with me about? Is it one of the horses?"

"No, sir," Jim answered. In his mind, he could almost hear Rose's snort, when she'd mentioned how her father's horses were more important than almost anything else to him. He tended to agree.

Had he paused a moment too long? His boss raised an eyebrow, and Levi took a breath. "I received a letter from home," he said. "My father is—" his voice cracked. He couldn't believe it. An unfamiliar stinging in his eyes pricked at him.

Taking a deep inhale, he got control over himself. "He doesn't have long the doctor says. I'd like to say goodbye. Just in case."

Mr. Alden nodded slowly. "I understand." He looked at the pregnant mare thoughtfully. "I know you'll think this isn't fair, Patterson, but I can't let you go till the mare delivers. There's no one else here who can assist and ensure as great a chance of survival for both horses. I need you."

Levi nodded. It was true. "I understand," he said.

"The moment she's delivered and upright, you have my leave to go. I'll have the men take over afterward, and hold down things until you return." He hesitated then. "I know you can't tell me when that will be, and I understand you'll have travel time. Can you try to be back within two weeks?"

Levi nodded.

"Good. I'll check in when the foal is born. Then, you can leave." Mr. Alden left, and Levi felt the tightness in his chest ease.

Jim walked in the barn a moment later. "I heard it all," he said, holding up a hand. "Don't you worry, boy, I'll take good care of those horses, as best as I can, and try and keep your spot here."

"Thank you," Levi said.

He finished his chores, his mind on anything but the horses. He didn't know what would be waiting for him back home, and he was scared to find out. It had been so long since he'd been home. What kind of welcome would there be? Would he even arrive in time?

There was so much uncertainty, and it wasn't something he enjoyed feeling. Levi had enjoyed the last few years of being on his own. He didn't have to rely on anyone but himself. At any moment, if he didn't feel right about something he could walk away. It was a good feeling, and one he wasn't anxious to give up.

He left the barn for a few minutes to head back to the bunkhouse. He grabbed his bedroll and a meal, then headed back to the barn to wait. Since it wouldn't be much longer, it wasn't wise to leave the mare alone. While a mare could give birth without assistance, it was still important to be there if there was an emergency. Making sure the stall was cleaned afterward was also important.

As many horses became protective and agitated after giving birth, it would be important that he stay close, as he was the most familiar to the mare.

Levi walked past Ruby, then stopped to rub her neck. The horse let out a snort, ducking her head. "I miss her too, girl," he said. Then looked around quickly when he realized he'd spoken aloud.

He laid his bedroll out, set a lantern nearby, and opened the book he'd been reading. In the nearby stall, the mare began to stamp her feet. She was getting restless. That meant it would be soon. He peered up at her, offering soothing words. "There, girl. You are fine. Going to be a mama soon. Just take it easy."

Remembering Mr. Alden wanted to know when it was almost time, Levi ran to the bunkhouse, as it was closer, and asked one of the men to take word to the house, then hurried back to the barn. The horse's water had broken. He waited anxiously.

Mr. Alden appeared a short time later. "How long ago did the water break?" he asked.

"Fifteen minutes," Levi answered, tension filling his body. He tried to remain calm, he couldn't let the mare sense his worry. He had plenty of it though. If the foal didn't come out soon, that meant something was very wrong.

"Will you be ready to help pull it out if it's not here soon?" Mr. Alden asked. Tense lines had formed on the man's face. Levi understood though. The mare had fetched a hefty price and the foal was extremely valuable. In this business, those were important things. The man's livelihood was tied up in the success of his horses.

"Yes, sir," Levi said, and then pointed. "She's trying."

Indeed, the mare was. The mare had started to roll, side to side, shifting the foal within her. The foal was emerging, though slowly. Levi swallowed. This was the dangerous part. He was ready though, even at risk to himself, to save the foal and the mare if he needed to. That was why he was paid so well.

There was a tension filled moment. By now, the barn was filling with the hands, each of them waiting silently, holding their breath. Levi had just decided to don his gloves and head in when the foal slid out, and the mare nosed it.

There was a collective sigh of relief. "Now, we wait for it to stand and nurse," Levi said. "If she doesn't nurse the foal within an hour, we need to help it."

Mr. Alden nodded. They waited, and soon the foal stood onto wobbly legs and latched on.

Wild grins broke out among the hands. Mr. Alden slapped Levi on the back, and accepted the whispered congratulations and handshakes from the hands. They were all quiet, so that the mare and her foal didn't startle.

"I'll stay the night," Levi said, "watching for the afterbirth. Then I'll get the stall all cleaned up for her."

There was a short nod from Mr. Alden, who had hardly taken his eyes off the foal. It was a beautiful charcoal gray. Both its parents were black. The hope was as the foal aged and its coat grew to the true color, it would be a solid black as well.

"Tomorrow, you can leave," Mr. Alden said. "There's a morning train at eight. Try to be back in two weeks."

"Yes, sir," Levi said. "Thank you."

Mr. Alden turned to him then. "You're a fine wrangler. I don't think I could replace you if I tried. You've broken Sadie in, nearly gotten Daphne used to the bit, saved Jade's hoof, birthed a valuable foal, and I rather appreciate a man like you being in charge of my horses. Just wish I had a few more like you."

It would have been impossible to stop the surge of pride that ran through Levi at the words. He didn't mean to be prideful, but the words meant a lot. All he wanted to do was be with the horses, and train others how to be firm but gentle with the beasts, teaching them to be whatever the owner needed. To do that for a living was a dream he hoped one day to accomplish, as the wrangler perhaps trained the trainers.

"Thank you, sir," Levi managed.

Mr. Alden met his eyes. "Good luck. I hope all goes well for you."

Wordlessly, Levi nodded. He hoped so too. In fact, at this very moment, there were only three things he wanted. If he could have them all, he'd never ask for anything more.

To spend his days doing what he loved, reconcile with his father before it was too late, and to kiss Rose Alden once again.

As the final thought came into his mind, he felt his eyes widen as his heart started pounding.

Where did that thought come from?

Chapter 15

Rose nibbled on the pastry she'd gotten at a brief train stop. A woman had been set up near the platform, and Rose and several others had rushed off to buy something to eat before dashing back to their seats. She was glad she'd bought several things. The train ride was expected to take two days. Luckily, she wouldn't have to take a stagecoach, the train arrived in her aunt's town.

It was bad enough being on the train, but at least she could walk to stretch her legs if she desired, unlike a cramped stagecoach, shoved in with others as tightly as they could fit.

The scenery had changed quite dramatically as they rode. At first, it was much the same. Plains, small towns sprinkled throughout the flat areas, and in the distance tall mountains in deep blues and purples rose. Though it was summer, snow still glinted on the tops. It really was beautiful, but she enjoyed each time the scenery changed. With so little to do on the train, it was nice to have a new view now and again.

The young child sitting behind her started kicking her seat again. Rose pressed her lips together. Her backside was sore and her back ached from the train bench. The kicking only made it worse. When she'd twisted around once before, she'd seen a very weary mother and so decided just to endure.

That seemed to be her motto as of late. *Endure.*

Her mind drifted to Levi, and not for the first time that trip. As she recalled his story, she wondered at how much heartache he'd felt. Did men feel heartache the same way that women did, she wondered. When he'd spoken of his past, of his parents and the expectations laid out for him, she'd only sensed bitterness. That, she understood.

When he'd mentioned the woman he had loved, there wasn't a wistfulness, but almost...an anger. Was it possible he felt used? Unwanted, by the fact that the woman, Carol, had willingly gone to another man without any argument at all?

That wouldn't have been her. If it had been a man she loved, she'd have fought for him.

But love...what did she know of love? She'd never really felt it before. Rose pondered the question and recalled Levi's lips pressed to hers. She felt her cheeks warming, and let out a soft sigh. She could almost, almost feel the warmth of his breath on her face, the pressure of his lips against hers. After the kiss, they had just sat. Neither had said much, but it was the most comfortable thing she'd ever felt. She didn't have to talk, didn't have to be anything but herself.

Was... that love?

But as soon as the thought came to her, she shook it off. It didn't matter now, did it? She was being sent away, and the next time she saw Levi—if she ever got to see him again—she'd belong to another man and his kisses, so sweet, so tingly, so wonderful, wouldn't be for her.

Rose's vision got blurry, and she realized with surprise her eyes were filled with tears. Yes, this must be love. But would she ever feel it again?

The drumming of the child behind her on her seat pulled her from her thoughts, as her eyes scanned once more, unsuccessfully, for another seat to move into. Thankfully, the train would arrive tomorrow. She just had to survive a little while longer.

Rose settled herself in as best as she could, and with her head against the glass window dozed off and on for the night. In the morning, she had another pastry and was overjoyed when the train released half of its passengers, and the ticketmaster told her they'd be arriving in just a few hours.

As she ate her last pastry, Rose couldn't entirely dismiss the feeling swelling in her stomach. It was almost a kind of excitement. It bothered her that dread could feel almost the same, making it hard to distinguish which she was feeling.

Rose kept her eyes trained to the window, and at last the train pulled into the station. As she got out, feeling exhausted from sitting for so long and a restless, uncomfortable sleep, she heard a throaty, "Rose! Dear girl, over here."

As she turned, Rose caught sight of her aunt Rosemary. Though it had been at least two years since she had seen her last, her aunt hadn't changed one bit.

"Aunt Rosemary," she smiled, and took the offered hand for a squeeze.

Her aunt looked her over carefully. "You look exhausted. Come, they are preparing a bath for you at home and a proper meal. Your trunks are being taken to the house."

"Thank you," Rose said, hoping her words encompassed everything. She followed her aunt to a carriage and sat, her back perfectly straight, on the short drive.

"It's good to have you here, Rose," her aunt said. "I have been tasked with finding you a husband." She seemed to notice Rose's sudden stiffness and smiled. "There, there, dear. I will find someone suitable. I assure you that. I have all of the requirements from your parents. In the meantime, starting tomorrow, we shall take walks together, tea often, and I will make introductions to potential suitors. Oh yes, your parents will not be disappointed at all."

Rose couldn't stop herself. She asked, "But what of me, Aunt Rosemary? Will I be disappointed?"

Her aunt's eyebrows raised in surprise. "What a question. No, Rose. I shall endeavor to find you a suitable husband. Perhaps even one that you'll like. However, you must know you've not made it easy on your parents."

Her lips pressed together, Rose nodded, and let her gaze fall into her lap. The carriage came to a stop and she climbed out after her aunt.

The town house looked much the same. It was set just a short distance from the main street of the town. The house was two stories, painted white with a large porch, and, unless her aunt had changed things, was filled with overly fussy and not very comfortable furniture inside.

When her aunt opened the door, Rose smiled to herself. All seemed the same. There was a parlor with an overstuffed settee, several chairs, and a table between with other smaller tables throughout the room. Large bouquets of fresh flowers sat on the tables.

"It looks lovely, as always," Rose said. And then she breathed in deeply. "Something smells wonderful."

Her aunt smiled in pleasure. "I recall that you liked stuffed chicken? I had Cook make some, along with baked apples and mashed potatoes. After you bathe, come join me in the dining room and catch me up on how your parents are."

"Yes, Aunt Rosemary," Rose said. So far things were starting off well. She hoped it would be a good sign of things to come. Rose stepped toward the stairs and rested one hand on the banister. "Am I to have the same room as last time?"

Her aunt nodded. "Yes, the third on the right. The bath should be all ready. Please let Clara know if you need something."

Clara was her aunt's maid. She was nearly as old as Aunt Rosemary was and just as proper, but a kind woman who had looked after Aunt Rosemary from the time she had married some forty years ago and all through the grieving time of her husband's death nearly two decades before. She was always there, but had a gift of blending in and not being seen unless she was wanted.

As Rose removed her dirty travel dress and lowered into the steaming water, she wondered. What if Aunt Rosemary's husband had never died? She'd never met him herself, but had understood theirs was not a love match. If he was around, would she still have been so determined to be in everyone's business?

It made her wonder if her aunt's fascination with everyone and what they did had come about because she herself had never gotten to choose what she wanted in a husband, and this was her way of exacting some control over others.

As Rose ducked under the water to remove the grime from her hair, she knew one thing was certain. It didn't really matter at all how her aunt was.

All that mattered was in just a few short days, she'd be introduced and likely married off to a man she had no interest in.

Chapter 16

Levi stood outside of his parents' house, hat in his hand. He had stopped on the way and bought a suit. He couldn't very well appear in his work clothes. His mother would likely call for her smelling salts.

Tugging on his collar, he wondered how he'd ever worn clothes like this daily. It had been a while, but he recalled never enjoying them, yet never feeling to suffer as much as he was now. Perhaps it was because he was also nervous.

As he studied the large door before him, trying to get the courage to summon a knock, Levi wondered just what was beyond the door.

A welcome? Or something else?

He raised his hand to knock when the door opened, and he stumbled forward. His sister, Megan, stood there, and then flung herself at him. "Levi! Levi, I've missed you!"

Levi returned her hug, and as he pulled back, he searched her face. "Father," he asked, swallowing hard. "Is he..."

"He's in his study," she said. "He's sitting up today. The doctor says that's a good sign."

A surge of relief went through Levi. "Thank goodness," he muttered.

"Come in," Megan told him. "The neighbors will talk if you just stand there."

He followed her in and shut the door. "How did you know I was outside?"

"I'd been watching you through the window for several minutes," she said. Then she smiled sympathetically. "I thought I'd help you find the door."

Levi opened his mouth to give a retort, then saw the tease in her face. He laughed instead. "And Mother?"

"She's at a ladies meeting," Megan said.

He frowned then. "With Father so ill?"

Megan shrugged. "He insisted," she answered. "You know how Mother can be."

Levi nodded. He did. She would have fussed and wrung her hands, and fluttered about carrying on terribly. Prone to bouts of anxiety, doing something outside of the house was likely the best thing for her.

"Should I go in?" he asked. Tension filled his body. What was he going to say? To do, when he finally saw his father.

Megan rested her hand on his arm and gave a small squeeze. "I think that's a good idea," she said. "I'll send in some refreshments."

"No need," Levi said. "I doubt I'll have an appetite."

She just smiled and watched as his leaden feet dragged him to his father's study, where he knocked on the door.

"Come in," his father's familiar voice called out.

Levi pushed open the door. His father looked up. There was a long, strained moment between them, then his father spoke again. "Well, come in. Don't stand there."

Nodding, Levi walked in further. "Hello, Father," he said, and studied him in the same way his father was staring at him.

It was obvious his father was tired. His color was off, but he seemed much the same as he had years before—fit, a formerly athletic form softening only slightly with age, and intelligent eyes that could pierce through a lie but soften at a patient's needs.

His father sighed, breaking him from his observation. "Sit down. Don't stand and make me strain my neck. I'm sure you've heard, I'm not well."

"I have," Levi said, his voice low. "That's the only reason I came."

"It's good to know that you've at least some feeling of affection in your heart for your parents," his father said wryly.

Levi remembered his sister's letter, and a line floated back into his memory. *You are still their child and they love you dearly.*

There was a soft knock, and Megan came in, deposited a tray, and left, closing the door behind her. His father inspected the tray. "Good. I was hungry. Megan always knows, somehow."

"She's gotten that from you, I suspect," Levi said. "The second nature of how to care for someone."

"I did what I thought was right by her," her father said quietly. "As I tried to do with you. No matter. A man must make his own way. A woman can not. Society dictates and we are the slaves. Your sister understood, and she has found a measure of happiness. Now, tell me, what do you do? You've four years to fill me in on. And I want to hear it all."

"Are you certain?" Levi asked doubtfully. So far, this was not going how he'd thought. He'd expected anger and an argument before he'd scarcely said hello. Not...a conversation.

"Of course. It's likely you've had adventures you'd not want your mother to hear about, but I'd find interesting. Best to let those out while she's gone."

Levi had to laugh. His father was right. He picked up a cookie his sister had brought in, and bit into it. With a nod, he chewed, then said, "Where to start?"

"With what you are doing now," his father said, leaning forward almost eagerly.

Though his sister had said his family was aware of where he was, he wasn't sure how much they knew. As much as he longed to say something, he wouldn't out his sister like that, and if his father was fading away, this wasn't the time to bring up hurt feelings. So, instead, he finished the cookie and said, "I work for a wealthy rancher. I'm his wrangler."

"Wrangler." His father frowned and looked confused. "We don't use that word around here. That means you work with his horses? A ranch hand?"

"Kind of," Levi said. Then he explained, "Wrangling is more than just being a ranch hand. It requires special training. I'm responsible for the horses only. Their care, their training. I break them in, even helped a few days back in a foaling. It was my responsibility to ensure the safety of the mare and her foal."

He couldn't keep the pride out of his voice when he continued, "It was the foal of two thoroughbreds, one a racehorse, and already there was a buyer for a thousand dollars."

His father stared at him, almost gaping. "A thousand dollars?"

Levi laughed as he shook his head. "Some of these rich people have no qualms about that. It was imperative the foal survive, and I had taken full responsibility for it.

That's what I was hired to do. Thankfully, all was well, and my boss was quite pleased."

"It sounds like a special set of skills needed to do all of that," his father said. "How did you learn it? You didn't grow up around horses."

"That's another story," Levi said.

"I'd like to hear it," his father said. He met Levi's eyes. "It might be hard for you to believe, my son, but I have missed you. And I want your success and happiness in life."

Levi swallowed hard against the lump in his throat. "Thank you, sir," he said. At his father's expectant look, he started his story. "Right after I left, I traveled for a little, but did a lot of listening. One night, I heard a man in a diner trying to explain the differences in bits for horses to a stable hand. The hand didn't care. But for some reason, I found it fascinating, and asked if I bought them some pie and coffee, could I join the table and listen. Three hours later, I looked up when the diner owner said they were closing. The farm hand had left, but the man, Mike Smith was his name, and I were still talking."

"Sounds like it must have been quite a conversation," his father said with a raised eyebrow.

"I learned more from that slice of pie and cup of coffee in those hours than I'd ever known about how particular types of bits should be used, when they should be used, and the benefits of one type of rein over another."

Levi paused for a breath and a sip of his mug. It was fresh cider, and he drank deeply. "Next thing I know, we met for lunch, and spent the whole day together. Turned out the guy was a former trainer. He'd worked for families in Europe and the United States with their race horses. He was incredibly sought after for his knowledge."

"And he spent all that time with you?" His father didn't hide the surprise, but that was okay, Levi had felt that way too.

"I know! I was a nobody. But I enjoyed it so much, I followed him around for a year. He taught me everything. I became his assistant and while I didn't make much money, I more than made up for it with knowledge."

Levi shook his head then, a flash of anger filling him. "There needs to be more education for horse owners. Do you know, people put their horses to slaughter too soon because they don't care for them properly? They damage the horse's hooves and teeth, their noses, leaving permanent scars because they don't know better. They aren't trained properly in animal use, so that the animal can be used in the setting they are desired for."

Passion had filled him now as he paced about the room. "Some of these owners expect a horse to do everything—pull a plow, pull a carriage, be ridden in races—without realizing that each of these things is a specialized skill the horse should be trained for to maximize their potential and outcome. So many foals die, a terrible waste, because of simple and sanitary precautions that could have been taken. The same with yearlings. An animal doesn't always need the whip to learn."

Levi stopped suddenly. "Forgive me. You aren't interested in that."

"No," his father agreed, "Horses are not my passion. But it appears they are yours. It also appears that what you are suggesting is that there needs to be far more trainers."

Levi sat again. "There does need to be. I'd like, with my boss's permission, to teach one of the young boys around the place who seems to have a knack. A person in the town asked the same, for himself and his son."

"A man could make a business out of it," his father said with a raised eyebrow.

"I would like that one day," Levi agreed.

Just then, the door opened, and his mother came into the room. She stared at him for a long moment, then tearfully said, "I will not embarrass you or myself by rushing at you, but it does your mother's heart good to see you are well." She sank down in a nearby chair. "Megan, I must have my smelling salts," she said.

Levi tried not to smile at her dramatic reactions. His mother held a hand to her head as she leaned back. "It's good to see you, Mother," he said, and gently patted her hand. "Should I see you helped to your room?"

"Yes, the shock. It's so great," his mother mumbled as she sat there. Levi motioned to one of the servants who stood close to his mother, offering his arm as a support. She took it and glanced at Levi. "I will see you at dinner though. Don't leave."

She left the room and Levi looked back at his father.

"Some things never change," his father said. But then, with a thoughtful look, added, "Yet others do. My boy, I wish to rest. There's something important I want to talk to you about after dinner."

Levi nodded and left, closing the door behind him. The house was silent, and he went to his old room. It looked the same as he'd left, and he spent an hour looking through it, wondering at his father's cryptic remark.

What had he meant? What had changed?

Chapter 17

Rose stifled a sigh. Evidently, her manners were not quite up to snuff, and her aunt had made her practice her small talk, explained the "importance" of taking small steps, the way she held her teacup, and even schooled her in the way she must nibble delicately on a cookie—only one, never more—until she was weary.

She'd had visits with several of her aunt's friends, and had sat there miserable and hardly talking. How anyone could spend days eating a crumb at a time was beyond her. She was hungry, and tonight planned to help herself heartily at supper, her aunt's approval or not.

Alone, but for who knew how long, she hoped that she'd be able to rest just for a moment. With a yawn, Rose leaned back in the plush champagne crushed velvet chair and closed her eyes. Maybe if she thought hard enough, she could imagine herself back at home, upon Ruby's back, the wind in her hair.

Smiling now, Rose could feel the sun beating on her, hear the small nearby creek trickle, and smell the fresh grass. She'd give anything to be there in truth, even if it was just for a few moments.

She'd hardly had a moment to herself since she arrived. Like before, nothing was done without her aunt nearby. If she wanted to read, or have a cup of tea, or go for a walk, or even just breathe, her aunt was right there, watching her with eyes that were sharper than any hawk.

Being by herself was bliss, and something she'd never take for granted again. Everything was calm. Still. Serene.

"Posture, Rose!"

The throaty voice of her aunt made her sit up quickly. "I'm sorry, Aunt Rosemary," she said. "I just—"

"A lady never 'justs'. A lady is, at all times—"

"A lady," Rose finished. At her aunt's approving smile, she took the smallest of sips of tea, holding it just so, the way her aunt had insisted on.

"Good, good," her aunt said. Then she walked excitedly about the room.

"You seem delighted about something," Rose said, trying not to let her aunt's mood concern her more than it was. Her aunt only seemed to smile when she was scheming or gossiping.

Her aunt clapped her hands and held them in front of her, clasped near her heart. "I am. I have four young men lined up for you to meet. You will have tea together in my parlor. The first arrives tomorrow."

"Must I?" Rose objected. "I've only just arrived."

"Nonsense. You've been here three days now," her aunt scolded. "I've gotten inquiries as to why you are a recluse. No, you will do as your parents have requested, and meet these young men."

"Might I at least know who I am meeting?" Rose asked.

"Yes, good idea," her aunt agreed, and produced her book that contained the detailed of account of everyone she knew. She flipped through the pages, and finally said, "The son of a doctor, the son of a politician, the son of a banker, and the son of a businessman."

Rose raised one perfectly arched eyebrow. "And why would any of those make for a good husband?"

The look her aunt fixed on her was one of pity. "Wealth, power, notoriety," she said with a delicate shrug. "Pick one. It doesn't matter." Then she frowned and tapped a page. "The only one I don't know much about is the son of the doctor. He's been traveling, I understand. No doubt to improve his own medical education."

"Wonderful," Rose said. "Then, when I throw up in disgust, he can treat me."

Her aunt gasped. "Rosemary Alden. Such language! Go to your room immediately. When you can speak like a proper young lady, you can return."

Rose stood, all too eager to obey, when a sharp "Wait" halted her. Her aunt studied her carefully. "Clever, girl. You wanted to be sent away. No. Back to the lessons. Sit. Back straight. Arms relaxed. Calm, serene expression. We will practice your posture all night if we must. Your backward small-town ways will be wiped from you before tomorrow."

Rose gritted her teeth. Her aunt was too perceptive. As she followed the endless commands, all she could think about was how much she missed home. She missed Ruby. She missed riding. She missed Levi.

Would she ever see him again? If she did, would he even care about seeing her? Perhaps all of her thinking about him was one sided. After all, Levi knew as well as she did that a romance between the two of them could never be. Her father would forbid it.

It wasn't just that Levi was hired help. He was also a wrangler, talented though he might be. She was the daughter of a wealthy man. It was expected that she marry well to continue that.

Which was why she was here, unenthusiastically preparing for her future husband. As her aunt thumbed through her book, making comments about this man or that, Rose only half paid attention. She was worried about meeting these men. What if they were all horrible? Surely, they couldn't expect much of her domestic abilities. Cooking wasn't something she was capable of; she'd also never had to do it. But any of these men would have money, which would mean a housekeeper or cook or both.

A sigh escaped then. Was she really even thinking about that? She was betraying herself. What about not wanting to get married? What about trying her best to get out of it? Rose bit her lip. The problem was that she'd never get a chance. Her aunt was always, always there.

The book her aunt held closed with a snap and she smiled broadly at Rose. "Doesn't that sound wonderful?"

Rose had no idea the question, but she formed a smile in return, and nodded, hoping there wouldn't be a follow up question.

"The next few days will be quite unforgettable," her aunt sighed happily. "You have opportunity before you, Rose, dear. You must not squander it. Enjoy each moment as it comes. Soon, everything will change for you."

The words, spoken with absolute joy in her voice, filled Rose with a sudden fear.

Yes. Everything would change. And none of it for the better. The hallway clock struck, and its chime served to remind her that her time as a free woman was almost at an end.

Chapter 18

Much to Levi's surprise, dinner was relaxed. He wasn't hounded with questions. Instead, his mother chatted about this person and that, and his sister told little stories about her children. In some ways, it was like he'd never left. No one made mention of his absence or his new job. It was strange in a way, but he accepted it as what appeared to be a peace offering and a gift for his return.

His father had managed to make it to the dining room table. Levi hoped it wasn't his imagination that his father looked slightly better. No one had even told him yet what was ailing his father. He didn't want to ask his mother—she'd likely say something about it being a broken heart from him leaving.

At the table, his mother fluttered over his father, while his sister calmly helped him as needed. His father tried to shoo them away, but it was obvious he was exhausted.

Throughout the meal, Levi observed the unique change in dynamics. He'd have never believed such a thing. Maybe people could change. He'd heard it was possible, though for his own family, he doubted such a thing. Perhaps he was wrong. It would be nice if he was. A part of him was waiting for everything to change, but he tried not to think about that.

"How is your husband? Your children?" Levi asked his sister. "You shared stories of them, but why did they not come?"

Megan smiled. "He is doing well. The children are with their other grandmother right now, while Douglas is busy at work. He's the manager over eight banks now, if you can believe it. He travels at times. Sometimes I go with him."

Levi nodded. He wanted to ask her if she was happy. If giving up her dream had ever lost the sting it once had, but he couldn't bring himself to do so. Not with their parents around. Again, he likened her situation to Rose's. Would she ever recover from her forced marriage? It wasn't any of his business, a fact he was keenly aware of, but it didn't stop him from wondering.

Megan had always been a confidant, and he hoped he'd be the same if something was upsetting her or if she wasn't happy. His sister deserved happiness.

However, it was as if she knew what he was thinking. Megan reached a hand out and softly said, "All is well, Levi. I have not given up on my passion. The time will come for it. You should not be distressed either." She was quiet a moment, and Levi observed his parents talking, not noticing his clandestine conversation with Megan. She leaned close, her voice low. "Things have changed. You were the catalyst."

He wanted to ask more, but his mother chose the moment to ask him a question. "Are you taking good care of yourself? Are you getting enough sleep?"

It was so ridiculous of a question, considering the circumstances, it was all he could do not to laugh. But he politely answered, "Yes, Mother. I am."

Satisfied, she smiled at him, offering him a second slice of pie, which he happily took. Their cook had never had a complaint made against her by him.

Dinner passed quickly, and Levi helped his father back into his study. His father was moving slowly, stiffly. He settled into a chair and waved Levi away when he hovered.

"Shut the door, son. I want to talk with you. Your mother knows what I have to say, we've discussed it, but I thought you'd prefer to hear this from me instead of her, in her agitated state."

Levi instantly felt nervous. Was his father about to tell him he only had hours left? Days? He sat, but nearly on the edge of his chair, his attention all on his father.

"Levi," his father began, "we've wasted a lot of time. But that time has given me the chance to ponder many things regarding the ways of life. I've made a decision. I know you wish to be your own man. However, I also want to see my boy happy. Settled, even."

"Settled?" Levi asked.

"Yes. With a woman. Perhaps a few small ones running in the yard, getting taught about horses by their father."

Levi wasn't quite sure how to answer that. He'd never really thought that far ahead, but now that his father had planted the idea, it didn't seem half bad. Maybe his children would love horses as much as he did. What age could you gift a pony? Perhaps four? Five?

His thoughts were broken up as his father continued. "I know after Carol—"

"I'd rather not talk about that," Levi said, his head snapping upward. "My heart has healed, but I've no wish to bring up the past."

It was quiet, then his father nodded. "Very well. But your mother is distraught that she's never had the chance to make introductions to young ladies for you. And I, though I realize you will not pick up my stethoscope when I am gone, I am disappointed that I might never bounce a grandchild you give me on my knee."

"I don't quite follow," Levi said.

"Married, boy! We want you to get married."

His father had seemed to come to life then, but the effort had been great, and he leaned back. "While I'm not near my death bed, and in my heart I think I will recover from the illness that weakened me, I'd like you to suppose I am, and grant an old man a dying wish."

Levi frowned then. Had this been a ploy to get him home? There was no denying his father looked poorly, but he didn't think he would be leaving the earth any time soon. Yet before he could ask, his father had held up a hand.

"My being ill wasn't done to trick you to get home. But while you are here, should you run off again tomorrow, or the next day, as I know you must eventually to get back to work, will you do just one thing for your mother and me?"

"What is that?" Levi asked.

"I want you to do me a favor, for your mother's sake. A few doors down, a friend of your mother's would like you to make the acquaintance of a lovely young lady. Your mother told her you were home visiting and were unmarried."

His father held his hand up again, stalling any objections. "I've quite made up my mind this is all to be your choice. But if you would humor us—especially your mother, if for nothing else, my sake. Just a simple visit, nothing more, then I promise your obligation to meet women of our choosing is complete."

"Would it be, though?" Levi asked. "Would it really? Mother would accept that? You would accept that?"

His father nodded. "As I said, things have changed. When you left, we thought we lost you. It made me stop and evaluate everything. My family is more important than anything else. I realize how I placed lofty ambitions upon your shoulders and it wasn't right. You'd have never been happy as a physician. But as a wrangler, you seem quite content."

"I am," Levi agreed. He sat quietly for several moments, thinking over what his father had asked. Finally, he said, "May I think it over tonight? It's been a long day, and I'm tired."

"Of course," his father said. "Go rest. Come see me in the morning."

Levi nodded, rested a hand on his father's shoulder, and left the study. As he changed his clothes for bed, he looked around the room once more. A collection of his old books still sat on a shelf, and he picked up one, settled on the bed, and started to read it. His eyes grew heavy, and the next thing he knew, the rising sun beaming through the window was near blinding him.

He rubbed at his eyes, and yawned, then caught sight of the book in his hand. He placed it back on the shelf, hurriedly got dressed, and made his way downstairs.

Megan was helping their father to the table. He seemed to be moving better, but it was obvious he was at the stage where he could overdo things and send himself right back to bed. "Can I help?" Levi asked.

"Just pull out his chair," Megan suggested.

Their mother came in, kissed him and Megan, then sat. Cook served breakfast, and everyone ate. Levi was quiet. The chatter at the table didn't involve him. However, what did was the heavy question he had to answer. Though he'd promised his father to consider visiting the young woman down the street, he'd been so tired, he fell asleep without even a moment's thought to whoever the woman was and if he really wanted to call on her or not.

Perhaps he should have asked questions about her. Maybe that would have made it easier to decide. Or would it have made it even harder to go if he knew what was waiting for him?

Knowing his mother, she was some flighty girl, with blonde hair, no personality, and entirely too meek for his liking. He wanted someone smart, witty, someone with gumption.

The word made him smile, and he thought about Rose. He hoped he would see her again. If nothing else, to make sure she was well. Happy. His heart sank. He wished he'd been able to spend more time with her. After their kiss, he knew without a doubt there was something incredibly special about Rose, and he wanted to experience it every day of his life.

Levi looked up. His mother was laughing about something, but it seemed forced. His sister was trying not to get caught staring at him. His father was watching him, and not even trying to hide it.

"Alright," Levi snapped, smacking the table. "I'll go see her. But I'm not making any promises, though I will hold you to yours, Father," he warned.

"Oh, my dear boy," his mother crooned, and clasped her hands together. "I am overcome with joy."

"Can you at least tell me what she's like? What I'm getting into?" Levi asked. He was scowling, he knew it. He also wasn't acting his age, but it didn't matter. If he had to go, it was reluctantly and he wanted everyone to know it.

His mother hesitated. That was not a good sign. It was obvious she was looking for the girl's qualities. By the long pause, she must not have any.

Finally, she said, "Well, she's tall, and likes to read."

"Go on," Levi said, spearing up a sausage link. "That's not much to go on."

"I met her at tea the other day. She was quite quiet. Shy, I believe."

"I see." Levi drank his water and then set the cup down. "She doesn't sound at all like the type of girl I want. But I will do this for you, Mother, Father, I promised I would. But only this once."

"You said she doesn't sound at all like the type that you want. Do you already have a girl in mind?" his mother asked, curiously. "I suppose we should have asked that already. I do apologize, dear. You hadn't mentioned anyone, so I just assumed..."

Levi hesitated, then admitted, his eyes trained on the remnants of his breakfast, "There is someone. But her father would never accept me. I'm not good enough for them."

To his surprise, his mother had tears in her eyes as she reached for his hand. Megan did as well. His father looked unhappy. Since when had his family become so sentimental?

His father cleared his throat and gruffly said, "Anyone who doesn't think my boy is good enough is obviously a fool."

The words and gestures and complete feeling of love that came from his family took Levi by such surprise, the lump in his throat that formed, this time, could only be described as gratitude.

The day passed slowly. Levi tried to fill time by listening to his mother's stories, and playing chess with Megan and his father, but it was no good, he was distracted, and after his sister beat him twice at the game, he just sat and watched her play his father.

Near mid-afternoon, he left the house, a ball of anxiety tight in his stomach and rattling around like a pebble in his favorite pair of boots that had a hole in the toe.

His mother had pointed out the house at least a dozen times since breakfast, so he knew it well by heart. It was not too far from theirs, so the walk only took about two minutes. He wished it was a longer one, but before long, he was on the front steps, a finger at his suddenly too-tight collar.

One thing was for sure. Levi was looking forward to going back to work and getting out of these stiff clothes and into something more comfortable.

He raised his hand to knock, and was let in by an older woman, who led him to a short hallway. She knocked on the door to what he assumed was the parlor, and then opened the door and motioned for him to walk inside.

Levi was directly across from a large picture window, and a young woman stood, her back to him as she looked out the window to the yard beyond. Levi glanced at her, but then gave his full attention to the woman who had her hand out and was walking toward him.

"It is good to meet you at last," she said. "I've heard so much about you from your mother."

"Thank you for inviting me to visit you," Levi said politely.

"We are delighted to make your acquaintance," the woman said. Please, allow me to introduce my niece."

A polite smile plastered on his face, Levi turned his head toward the woman before the window. It was obvious she wasn't interested in meeting him. Her posture was stiff, her hands were clenched at the side. She seemed nothing like the meek, docile woman his mother had described.

Long, dark hair flowed well past her shoulders. Levi held back a sigh, the sight of it making his heart ache for the woman he'd never seen again.

There was a knock on the door, and the other woman said something quietly to his hostess. "Forgive me, I must leave a moment," his hostess said, and scurried out of the room.

Uncomfortably, Levi stood. "Hello," he finally said.

The woman turned then, a storm cloud looking friendlier than her face, and upon catching sight of him gasped. Levi blinked several times. There was a jolt in his stomach. It couldn't be.

"Rose?"

Chapter 19

When the man she was supposed to meet walked in, Rose was angrily staring out the window. Her aunt having to leave was a blessing. This was her chance to send the man away running, as fast as she could.

He said hello, and she turned. Then froze. Lightheadedness came over her and she gasped, then reached out to grab the chair near her for support.

"Rose?"

The voice was filled with just as much surprise as she felt. Her heart felt like it was about to burst from her chest.

"Levi?" Her voice was barely a whisper. It cracked horribly.

But less than a moment later, Rose was in Levi's arms, and his lips were pressed to hers. She reveled in them, her arms clasping around him. She wasn't sure if she'd run to him or he had run to her or if it had been the both of them, but it didn't matter. Levi was here, *here!*

"I never thought I'd see you again," she gasped, touching his face to make sure it really was him. "What are you doing here?"

"I got a letter my father was ill. I came to visit him. Then he asked me to meet a young woman as a favor for my mother. Just one, they promised, and they'd never ask again." Levi pulled in her for another kiss, this one to Rose's forehead, where he breathed her in deeply.

"I almost said no. I almost said no." His voice sounded strange, a mixed up jumble of emotions and thoughts and all of it unable to be expressed properly. Somehow, it absolutely delighted her.

Rose looked up at him then. "I'm so glad you didn't." She sighed, and held him tightly, raising on her toes for another kiss.

"Good heavens!" A throaty gasp made Levi startle and spin around. Rose brought her hand to her mouth, but it wasn't in horror, but to suppress her giggle.

Aunt Rosemary stood there looking aghast, one hand to her bosom. She swayed for a moment, and Rose wondered if she might collapse on the spot. Her aunt's mouth opened for a moment wordlessly, before she found her tongue. "You young people don't waste any time now days, do you?"

Rose stepped closer to Levi and rested her hand on his arm. Levi slipped it around her, pulling her close. "You wanted me to pick a husband," she said. "I choose him."

"You'll have to choose him," her aunt agreed, bobbing her head frantically. "The window drapes were wide open. Half the town saw you. Your reputation will be in tatters." She twisted her fingers together. "Rose, of all the foolish things you could have done. I know you don't want to marry, but—"

"Forgive me," Levi interrupted. "It was I who kissed Rose. I couldn't stop myself."

"That's almost as bad," her aunt whispered, and collapsed into a chair. "What will we do? Oh! What will your father do to me?" She dropped her head into her hands, and Rose felt a twinge of guilt. She glanced at Levi and saw he felt the same.

"Fetch my parents," Levi suggested. "We will discuss it."

"Good idea," her aunt said, and springing up called in the hallway to her maid. When she returned, Rose and Levi were sitting close on a small sofa, holding hands.

"This has moved far faster than I imagined," her aunt said, highly agitated. "Though your father will be pleased. As long as he doesn't hear of this...wanton behavior."

"Not entirely," Rose said, her voice low. Now she was feeling quite worried. How could she say it? Straight to the point would be best. Rose took in a deep breath to steel herself. "There's something you must know, Aunt."

"Wait until the Pattersons are here," her aunt said. "I can only take shocks in small doses. I am old, dear, but I'd like to enjoy a few more years."

Rose nodded, and looked down again in her lap. Levi reached for her hand, and she smiled at him. Just his being there seemed to make her feel complete.

In a few moments, a man and woman Rose assumed were Levi's parents arrived. The woman was quite lovely, though she was wringing her hands constantly. The man, though pale, gave a hearty handshake to her. Once everyone had settled, her aunt spoke.

"I left the room for a moment, and when I returned..." she stopped, almost unable to go on. Her eyes closed a long moment, then she whispered, "They were in each other's arms and...kissing!"

Levi's mother gasped, and his father's eyebrows shot up. "Son?" he asked.

Levi stood then, pulling Rose up with him. "Mother, Father, this is Rose. She's the girl I love."

"You've only just met," Levi's mother said.

But his father had been watching, and then shook his head. "No, no, they haven't. Can't you see?" He took Rose's hand and gave it a gentle squeeze. "Is your father a wealthy rancher?"

Rose's eyes widened. "Yes. But then, I suppose Aunt Rosemary told you that."

"And is my boy your father's wrangler?"

Rose looked at Levi and moved closer. "Yes," she said. "And we've kissed, so we must marry, lest my reputation be ruined." To her surprise, Levi's father smiled, and his eyes seemed to twinkle.

"Oh my goodness," Levi's mother said, "What a disaster this is!" She fanned herself with a lace handkerchief.

"I don't understand," Rose said. "I was sent here to marry. Aunt Rosemary was to find me a husband. She has." She looked around at the others, confused.

"The problem, dear, is your father," her aunt said. "If he had been any other wrangler, but your father's..."

"You mean..." Rose's eyes filled with hot tears. "Do you mean I finally have someone that everyone would approve of, someone I love, and I can't be with him?"

Her heart was breaking, and she crumbled to the ground in sobs. Instantly, she was surrounded by Levi's mother and her aunt. They spoke soothing words to her, while Levi and his father were talking quietly. Sobs wracked Rose. It had been too good to be true. Now what?

"I have an idea," Levi's father said, his tone cutting through her tears, pausing them. Everyone stared at him. "Levi's skills are unique and rare and valuable. And he *is* still a doctor's son. But he's more than that now. He helped birth that thousand-dollar foal for your father. He could do that many more times. He could even train others to do the same."

"What are you saying?" Rose asked. Her eyes darted to Levi. He was holding her hand again, and pulled her to stand, but he also looked confused.

"I'm saying, I've got a fair bit of money. I'd like to invest it in you, Levi. Let you start that horse business you were talking about."

"No, you won't," a voice boomed from the doorway.

"Father?" Rose said. "How long have you been standing there?"

Her father crossed his arms. "Long enough."

Chapter 20

Levi jumped up to put himself between Rose and her father. "Sir, I—"

"I'm not talking to you, son," Rose's father said. He turned to Levi's father. "You mentioned a business proposal and horses. I want to hear what you have to say. Might be I want to be the one investing in that." He crossed his arms over his chest. "I am a businessman, after all."

Rose's mother had followed her husband into the room, looking quite bewildered. She sat near Rose's aunt and his mother. The women started to whisper, likely asking what was happening.

Levi didn't know what to think. He could hardly get his mind to work. Rose must have felt the same way. She was staring at her parents and then finally asked, "How did you get here? When did you get here?"

"It's not that we didn't trust you," Rose's mother said to her aunt. "We just wanted to make sure Rose wouldn't try to shirk her duty."

"Oh, she's more than guaranteed her marriage," her aunt replied. "They've... *kissed*."

Levi's mother rolled her eyes. It surprised him. "Isn't that what young people in love do?" she asked.

"Hush," Mr. Alden said. "I want to hear what Mr. Patterson was starting to say."

Levi's father shrugged. "It came to me last night. I don't know if you realize just how passionate Levi is about horses, and about making sure they are trained well and cared for properly."

"I do," Mr. Alden said, pulling up a chair. "That's why I hired him. He came well recommended, and he's proven himself in just the short time he's been with me." He paused, then added, "Your son is a fine man. Though, all that said, I'm not sure how I feel about my daughter being married to one of my ranch hands."

"I understand," Levi's father said. "But what about the fact he's a highly respected horse trainer, who is about to open his own place and take on others to train them?" With a nod to Levi, he added, "He's quite valuable in that regard. Why, when word gets around he helped ensure your mare and your thousand-dollar foal both survived a birth, what do you think will happen?"

Mr. Alden's nod was slow, even as his brow furrowed. "He'll have quite a reputation alright. Makes him valuable. That's not a skill many have." He looked up then, this time at his wife, "Makes us more important, being the one who has such a man in our employ. And if he were my son-in-law to boot...everyone knows he's off limits. That makes him, and me, even more important in this business." His eyes lit up as he talked it though.

"Sounds quite logical to me," Levi's father said, and then he winked at Levi.

Levi could hardly believe it. He wanted to jump in and say something, speak for himself, but he was so shocked that his father was boasting about him so much, he honestly wasn't sure he wanted him to stop.

"Takes a lot of capital to do something like that," Mr. Alden continued, rubbing at his beard. "Connections too. And recommendations."

Levi glanced at Rose. He knew that she didn't like the idea of being just an object to trade. It made him wonder if she thought poorly of him for not interrupting. Rose's eyes, however, were darting between the two, and the other women in the room were also watching closely.

With a nod, and a sharp look in his eye Levi remembered well, his father asked, "So, which part do you want to help with? I'm willing to invest my all in my son. I believe in him and his idea. What are you going to invest in your daughter? It's a father's prerogative to want the best for their child."

Rose tensed beside him, and Levi squeezed her hand to reassure her, though in truth, he could use a little reassuring himself. Was it possible that Mr. Alden was actually going to consider letting Rose be his wife?

A long moment passed, then Mr. Alden looked at Rose. "I know you think I only care about my horses. That's not true. So," he looked back at Levi's father, and then again to Rose, "I'm willing to invest as much into Levi and Rose as I am into my horses. My all. Whatever Levi and Rose need, that's what I'm giving."

Rose pulled away from him then, and flung herself at her father, tears falling down her cheeks. "Oh, Daddy," she sobbed, her voice muffled, "do you mean it? Does that mean that I can marry Levi?"

Her father looked at her with a smile on his face. Mrs. Alden was beaming, and tears were making her eyes glisten. Levi stepped forward then. "Only one more thing we have to do," he said.

Rose looked at him questioningly. Levi took her hand, brought it to his lips, and then sank to one knee.

Clearing his throat while staring at up her, he asked, "Miss Alden, would you do the honor of being not just my wife, but the only woman who I will ever love?"

Much to his surprise, Rose sank down next to him. "Yes," she said, throwing her arms around his neck. "Oh yes. I want nothing more."

Chapter 21

Rose could hardly believe it. Everything was almost settled and soon she and Levi would be starting their own life—one of their own choosing. Things had happened so suddenly, and she'd never expected such good fortune when she had arrived, but now...she was finally about to be with the man she wanted to be with.

Both her mother and Levi's, along with Aunt Rosemary, had been busy almost non-stop making wedding preparations. Even if she wasn't completely involved with them—her mother had ideas for days about what she wanted, Rose was actually okay with that. She had plans of her own she was making, those with Levi.

Freedom—the freedom of her own choice of husband, and one who understood her feelings and accepted and encouraged them—something she never thought she'd get, now seemed to overflow.

In fact, while the other women made the wedding plans, Rose more often than not found herself sitting between her father and Levi. Levi had included her in each detail of the plan he was formulating with his father and hers to build a business. Rose's ideas were welcomed by all, and more than once, her father had complimented her suggestions, mentioning proudly to the others she took after him with her business sense.

Her father had seemed to come alive in a way she'd never seen before, and even Levi's father's health seemed restored.

It was fascinating listening to Levi talk and each detail she absorbed eagerly. She learned about some of the best places to find quality horses, those that needed to be broken, the importance of care beyond grooming and feeding, and more details than she'd ever imagined when it came to running a business.

No wonder her father spent so much time thinking about horses and managing his affairs. There was far more to know than she currently knew, but she enjoyed each moment of it so far, and couldn't wait to learn the rest.

Spending this extra time with her father was amusing in many ways. The one thing she thought he loved more than anything else turned out to be the very thing that brought them together, and gave her the future she wanted.

Time flew, and before she realized it, Rose was in her aunt's backyard, staring at a sea of faces, her wedding bouquet tight in her hands. She knew almost no one there, but it didn't matter. The only ones she really wanted there were her family, Levi's family, and of course, Levi.

Rose's sisters and mother had helped her dress that morning, in a soft, ruffly, cream-colored dress that fluffed out near her ankles, though it was trim at the waist. A long row of buttons went up her back, most of them simply for show, and a delicately made lace at her throat and wrists set off the dress.

Seeing herself in the mirror moments before, Rose had to admit, she looked beautiful. Never had she thought she was until this moment. Her hair was swept up, with a pearl pin holding it in place, and she liked how it looked so much, she decided to wear it that way more often. Perhaps even in dresses similar to this one.

Music began to play, and Rose shook herself from her thoughts. Her father held out his arm, and Rose took it, tears filling her eyes.

As they walked down the aisle, every gaze on them, she thought to herself that just a few weeks prior she'd expected her wedding day tears to be ones of anger or sadness, not joy. The turn of events far exceeded her expectations.

Rose hardly listened as the reverend spoke. Her eyes were on Levi, who kept his only on her. Once pronounced husband and wife, they exchanged a kiss, turned, and were met with the cheers of the crowd.

The rest of the afternoon went by in a blur. There was a towering wedding cake with a raspberry filling, several kinds of fruity punches, and an assortment of finger foods and tiny sandwiches for the guests. Her mother, Aunt Rosemary, and Mother Patterson had outdone themselves, and Rose was delighted to have not had to worry about a thing.

As the sun started to dip, Rose and Levi bade their goodbyes, and quickly boarded the train that would take them back home, and to their new life. As it pulled from the station, Rose rested her head against Levi's shoulder. He dropped a kiss onto the top of it.

"When we get back and settled, I promise a proper honeymoon," Levi said. "You just tell me where you want to go."

"I don't need one," Rose assured him. "I'm just as anxious to get back as you are."

She opened her handbag and pulled out a sketch. As their wedding gift, her father had his men begin construction on a house for the two of them. Though it would be a short while before it was done, it was in the perfect location—near the wide-open pasture where she and Levi had their first kiss.

Levi moved close. "Right there," he said, pointing to the plot of land, almost as if he was able to sense her thoughts. "Right there is where I kissed you."

Rose looked up and smiled at him. "I think we should plant a tree right there. Make it our tree."

"I like that idea," Levi agreed. "I like all your ideas. Especially that one where you wanted to marry me."

She laughed then. "I'm glad you like a woman who knows her own mind," she teased.

As his arm pulled her close, Rose returned the sketch to her handbag, leaned against Levi, and reflected on how much more enjoyable this train ride was.

The train that had brought her to California had seemed to be taking her from the one thing she wanted. How funny that now it had led her to it, instead. Now, it was taking her right back to all she had ever wanted.

Had she changed? She wasn't sure. She knew her parents had. Levi said his parents had, and she would have quite a tale to tell one day to their children. Who'd have thought Rose Alden, daughter of one of the richest men in Oregon, not only romancing a wrangler, but marrying him too.

Epilogue

Four years later

Rose led Ruby around the pasture. On top of her, and safe in her mother's arms, three-year-old Marigold, named after her maternal grandmother, giggled.

"Faster, Mama! Faster, Ruby!" she encouraged.

"Not yet," Rose said. "First, you must start slowly."

"I see Papa," Marigold pointed.

"Yes, there he is," Rose said, and they rode slowly closer to the barn. In the corral beyond, Levi was with two of the young men he was training. He was pointing at the hooves of a horse, raising one and demonstrating something.

In just a very short time, Levi had become the go-to person when there was a horse question. Other wealthy horse owners had asked for him to train their stable hands and wranglers, and before long, Levi and her father had a successful partnership as men of all ages poured onto the Alden-Patterson ranch to learn from the best and paid handsomely for the privilege.

With that, also came travel at times, which Rose enjoyed very much. Their small family traveled to see the best horses, the newest equipment, and even to lectures about animal care. While enjoying those things, Rose also appreciated the chance to explore her own interests, and spend many hours in museums and browsing stores.

Her mother came with them sometimes, and enjoyed taking Marigold to children's amusements such as zoos and having picnic tea parties or long walks through parks.

Everything was going so well, Rose thought as she dismounted, helped Marigold off of Ruby, and the two of them rubbed her down. "Let's go back home for a bit," Rose said. "It's time for a nap."

Marigold crinkled up her nose, but didn't argue, the yawn escaping proof that maybe, just maybe, her mother was right.

As they walked along the creek leading to the hose, they passed a small tree with pink flowers on it. "That's your tree!" Marigold said.

"That's right," Rose agreed. "That's your papa and mine's tree."

"Will I have one?" Marigold asked.

"One day you might," Rose said with a smile. "That's not for a long way off yet. I'm in no rush for you to marry, and you shouldn't be either."

Marigold yawned again, and stretched out under the tree on a blanket Rose shook out. While her daughter napped, Rose read, until a shadow dropped over her book and she looked up, as a grinning Levi sat beside her.

"I thought I'd find you here," he said.

"It's my second favorite place to be," Rose told him, using her finger to mark her page.

"And the first?" Levi asked, curious.

"Anywhere you are," she told him, then tipped her face up for a kiss.

They separated a moment later and Levi said, "Wherever you are, I have all I want. Happiness, home, freedom, love...there's nothing better I could dream of."

Rose felt just the same, but she knew she didn't have to tell him that. They sat, backs against the small tree, and she reflected on all she had.

Really, nothing could be better. Except, perhaps, the look on his face when she told Levi that she was about to add to their family in a few months.

Note from Author

Thank you for taking the time to read Romancing the Wrangler!
Could I ask for one small favor? Reviews like yours on Amazon mean so much to me and help others to find my books! Even just a single line means a lot!

***

Want a FREE book?
Stop by my website to get your no strings attached **FREE book**. It's my gift to you, as a thank you for reading this book.
www.sarahlambbooks.com

About the Author

Sarah is wife to an amazing teacher and mom to two boys who are growing up just a little too fast. Her day job is helping others to become writers, while she squeezes in each spare moment she can on her own books. She spends her days working and writing in the Blue Ridge Mountains and planning her next trip to Disney World.

There are other great books in this series as well!

There are other great books in this series as well!

Find all them on Amazon!

https://www.amazon.com/dp/B0CFXVVLKP

www.ingramcontent.com/pod-product-compliance
Lightning Source LLC
Chambersburg PA
CBHW022019170626
46808CB00003B/987